Praise for Kate Hoffmann
from *RT Book Reviews*

The Charmer
"Hoffmann's deeply felt, emotional story is riveting.
It's impossible to put down."

Your Bed or Mine?
"Fully developed characters and perfect pacing
make this story feel completely right."

Doing Ireland!
"Sexy and wildly romantic."

The Mighty Quinns: Ian
"A very hot story mixes with great characters
to make every page a delight."

Who Needs Mistletoe?
"Romantic, sexy and heartwarming."

The Mighty Quinns: Teague
"Sexy, heartwarming and romantic...a story to
settle down with and enjoy—and then re-read."

Dear Reader,

I believe this book represents a milestone of sorts! *The Mighty Quinns: Kieran* is the 20th book in my Mighty Quinns series. Eleven years ago, my first Quinn book, *The Mighty Quinns: Connor,* hit the bookstores. It's still hard to believe I've been living with this extended Irish family for such a long time!

Since this is the second in a four-book series—and I've got four more planned for next year—I'm going to be living with them a little bit longer. Thank goodness they don't leave wet towels in the bathroom and dirty socks on my bedroom floor. But then, since I made them the people they are, I guess I could also suggest that they cook dinner and do the laundry whenever I wanted, too. But that's just wishful thinking....

I hope you enjoy this next installment in the Quinn saga!

All my best,

Kate Hoffmann

Kate Hoffmann

THE MIGHTY QUINNS: KIERAN

HARLEQUIN®
entertain, enrich, inspire™

Recycling programs
for this product may
not exist in your area.

ISBN-13: 978-0-373-79711-0

THE MIGHTY QUINNS: KIERAN

Copyright © 2012 by Peggy A. Hoffmann

www.Harlequin.com

Printed in U.S.A.

ABOUT THE AUTHOR

Kate Hoffmann has written more than 70 books for Harlequin, most of them for the Temptation and the Blaze lines. She spent time as a music teacher, a retail assistant buyer and an advertising exec before she settled into a career as a full-time writer. She continues to pursue her interests in music, theatre and musical theatre, working with local schools in various productions. She lives in southeastern Wisconsin with her cat, Chloe.

Books by Kate Hoffmann

Prologue

"Sometimes I wonder what really happened to them."

Kieran Quinn stared down at the section of weathered bright wood that he'd just sanded. He and his three brothers had had this same conversation over and over again during the past two years. And try as they might, they never came up with any answers to their questions.

The facts were simple. Their parents, Jamie and Suzanne Quinn, had been lost at sea, their boat disappearing somewhere between Seattle and the South Pacific. No one knew what happened, only that they were gone forever. Two years was a long time, but to Kieran, it felt like yesterday.

"Someday, I'm going to take this boat and try to find them," Dermot announced.

Though his twin brother had always been a dreamer and an optimist, Kieran had been given the practical genes in the pair. Dermot spent his allowance like he had a bottomless piggy bank. Kieran saved every penny. Dermot was the first one to jump, Kieran always looked very carefully before leaping. Dermot saw the possibilities in every situation while Kieran saw the pitfalls.

Kieran glanced over at the section of teak that Dermot had been sanding. It was rough and uneven. Even at work, Dermot favored speed over quality. But then, the four brothers were all different. It was hard to believe they came from the same parents.

Cameron, the eldest, was quiet and creative, so clever that he immediately knew exactly how to get a job done. Their baby brother, Ronan, was sensitive and compassionate, the kind of kid who stuck up for the underdog. Yet their brotherly bonds were unbreakable. They always stood together.

He and his brothers were in the process of restoring an old 22-foot sloop that had been abandoned at their grandfather's boatyard. Though their grandfather insisted that they were too young to take it out on their own, that didn't stop them. They'd been working on it for nearly a year, after school and on weekends, and had hoped to put it in the water to celebrate Cameron's fourteenth birthday.

"I used to think about it all the time," Cameron murmured. "Now, it just makes me sad. We're never going to figure it out."

"It makes me mad," Dermot said. "Why didn't they wait for us? Maybe if we'd been along, things might have been different."

"You really think so?" Ronan asked. Since the

accident, any mention of sailing made the youngest Quinn uneasy. He had stubbornly refused to set foot on a boat, making family sailing trips with their grandfather impossible.

Kieran felt a mixture of both—anger and sadness. Their lives would have been so much different had their parents lived. Instead of just surviving their grief, they'd be laughing and loving and enjoying every day. He'd seen each of his brothers change in significant ways, but he'd felt the change in himself the most.

He'd become cautious and careful. He wasn't willing to take any chances. He preferred his life to be perfectly ordered, so he knew exactly what to expect from day to day. He did his homework early, he completed his chores without complaint and he avoided conflict at every cost. It was hard to know what turns life would take, but Kieran did all he could to anticipate the future.

He didn't want to be unprepared again. Two years ago, he and his brothers had gone to the marina to wave goodbye to their parents. Their father had told Cameron to watch over his younger brothers and their mother had kissed them each goodbye, her eyes filled with tears. None of them had ever anticipated what was about to happen. Nor could they have been prepared for it even if they had.

When Jamie and Suzanne Quinn were a week late for their arrival, the boys and their grandfather were concerned but not worried. Many things could delay a trip seven days—broken rigging, the doldrums, a torn main sail.

But when a week stretched into two weeks and then a month, everyone was forced to face the truth. Something bad had happened. After a year, a funeral was held. The boys filled a single empty casket with memories of the parents they'd lost.

To help them deal with their grief, Martin Quinn put the boys to work at the boatyard. "Work will soothe a troubled mind," he told them. "Work will make you strong."

Martin had used work to get over his own grief many years before, when their grandmother had died in childbirth. Martin had come to the U.S. from Ireland two years later, a widower with his young son, hoping to make a new life for himself away from a homeland that held so many sad memories.

Dermot sat down next to Kieran and grabbed a worn piece of sandpaper. "I know they're dead. But what I really want to know is why."

"When we finish this boat, you can sail it across the ocean and find out," Ronan said.

Kieran drew a sharp breath. "This boat will never get out of the marina without sails. Where are we going to find the money to buy those?"

Cameron sat back on his heels. "We can maybe find something used. Still, we're all going to have to pitch in some cash." He looked at Dermot. "How much do you have saved?"

Dermot shrugged. "I don't know. Maybe twenty dollars."

"Ronan?"

"One-hundred-seventy dollars," the nine-year old said.

"Jaysus," Cameron muttered. "You're like a little squirrel."

Ronan grinned. "I count it every week. You can have it all."

"No," Cameron said. "We all have to contribute equally."

"That doesn't seem fair, considering Ronan is never going to go out on the boat," Kieran said. "He should contribute less."

His little brother shrugged. "I don't mind," he said in a quiet voice.

"How much do you have?" Cameron asked, turning to Kieran.

Kieran knew exactly what he had in the bank. He even knew how much he made every month in interest. And he knew that putting his money into sails for a boat they probably wouldn't be allowed to sail was foolish. He was saving his money for something more important—he just wasn't sure what that was. But someday, he'd need money and he'd be the only brother to have it.

"Enough," Kieran said.

"He knows," Dermot said. "He knows to the penny how much he has."

"Over a thousand," Kieran admitted. "But I'm not spending it all on this boat."

Cameron gave him a pat on his shoulder. "We decide as a group. And we all contribute the same. We're brothers."

Kieran nodded. "We're brothers," he murmured.

They'd all managed to survive together. But Kieran had to wonder how long that would last. Someday, Cameron would leave for college, perhaps in a place far away from Seattle. Dermot had big dreams of traveling the world. And Ronan would undoubtedly find a safe place for himself to settle.

But even if they were separated by distance, the four Quinn brothers had a bond that no one could break, a bond forged by a family tragedy and strengthened by a childhood spent watching out for each other.

"You know what we should do," Kieran said. "We should build ourselves a boat from scratch. Once we get this one fixed, we can sell it and build something we really like. Something bigger and better. After all, we got this boat for free and I bet, fixed up, we could sell it for fifteen thousand."

"Oh, man, that would be so cool," Dermot said. "Do you think Grandda would let us build our own boat?"

"Sure," Cameron said, clearly excited by the suggestion. "We'll tell him it will help us learn the business better. I've got some really cool designs we could look at. And when it's done and we're all old enough, we'll just leave."

"Where will we go?" Ronan asked, trepidation in his voice.

"The South Pacific," Cameron replied. "We'll go say goodbye to Ma and Da."

Ronan looked a little green at the thought. Kieran glanced over at his twin brother and their gazes met. Dermot understood. They just needed to feel what their parents felt, to see what they'd seen and then maybe, they could finally put the past behind them and build lives of their own.

1

"BITNEY, KENTUCKY? What the hell is in Bitney, Kentucky?" Kieran stared down at the bus ticket, shaking his head.

He and his three brothers had gathered in Cameron's office after a meeting with their grandfather. And they were all still trying to wrap their heads around what had just gone down. They'd suspected that Martin Quinn was thinking about retiring and turning over the control of the family yacht-building business to one of his four grandsons. But not one of them had expected this.

"So, let me get this straight," Dermot said. "We're supposed to walk away from everything here in Seattle for six weeks and find a new life for ourselves? In some strange place?"

Ronan nodded. "This is crazy. The old man has lost his mind. How the hell is he going to run this place without us?"

Kieran chuckled. "Don't worry about that. He

knows every job in the place. I swear, he could fire us all and the business would thrive."

Quinn Yachtworks had been started in the early sixties as a small fishing-boat repair business in Seattle. Their grandfather had gradually built it into the finest custom sailing yacht producer on the West Coast, known for its sleek, state-of-the-art designs.

Martin's only son, Jamie, had worked in the business until he and his wife, Suzanne, had been lost at sea.

It seemed as if every bit of happiness had leaked out of the young Quinns' lives on the day they buried that empty coffin. The things that made them a family had changed. There wasn't a lot of affection or laughter in the house. Instead, the boys worked and worked…and worked, pushing aside their emotions and their loss.

There had been some good moments, Kieran recalled. The four brothers had built a boat all on their own and he, Dermot and Cameron had spent an entire summer sailing it around Puget Sound, much to the dismay of Ronan, who refused to step on board. But the dreams they'd had for themselves as kids had been replaced by responsibility to their grandfather. Martin Quinn had taken them in when they needed a home. It was their family duty to repay him.

They all attended college locally and continued to work at Quinn Yachtworks, helping to expand the business even more. At first, they'd worked simple jobs around the shop and then, as they got older, they'd taken on more important positions. Cameron ran the design end and Dermot handled sales. Kieran served as chief financial officer and Ronan enjoyed supervising the shop, spending his days working side by side with the builders and craftsmen.

Yes, they'd all put aside their childhood dreams to help out after their parents' death. But it was silly to think any of them could go chasing after those dreams now. "Where are you going?" Kieran asked Dermot.

"Mapleton, Wisconsin." Dermot held up his phone, a tiny map on the screen. "It's not anywhere near water. Except for this little lake."

"Look up Bitney, Kentucky," Kieran asked.

"That's an easy one," Cameron said. "He's sending you to racing country. Remember how crazy you were about horses? You used to have all those plastic ponies lined up on your bedroom shelf. And you were always bugging Grandda to tell you about the horse he had when he was a kid. You even asked Da for riding lessons for your tenth birthday."

Kieran ran his hands through his hair and shook his head. "I barely remember that. I'd almost forgotten about Ma buying me those plastic ones all the time. She'd put them in my lunch box." He smiled at the memory. His mother had always been thoughtful like that. She'd loved playing with his horse collection as much as he did.

"Whatever happened to those ponies?" Dermot wondered.

"He wrapped them up and put them in the coffin," Cameron said.

"Right," Kieran replied. "I didn't think I'd ever want to play with them again. They reminded me too much of Ma."

A long silence grew between them.

"What time do you leave?" Ronan asked.

"Eleven-thirty tonight," Kieran replied. "I've got two and a half days on a bus. I can't imagine how much fun that's going to be."

Dermot chuckled. "You can catch up on your reading. Hey, it might be kind of cool. Who knows? I'm trying to keep an open mind. And a forced vacation isn't such a bad deal."

"Yeah, let's see if you feel that way after you've been stuck inside a bus for sixty hours," Kieran said. "Or you come back six weeks later to find your office buried in paperwork."

"Sixty hours? Look at mine," Ronan said. "Sibleyville, Maine. That's about as far away from Seattle as a guy can get. Three and a half days. That's one day more than any of you guys have."

Dermot held up his phone. "At least you'll be near water. Maybe you'll be able to find a decent job doing something you know about."

"What am I supposed to do in Vulture Creek, New Mexico?" Cameron asked.

"Well, at least that makes sense. Dinosaur bones. Remember? After you saw *Jurassic Park,* you started digging up the garden. Dinosaurs were all you ever talked about. And then you found that bone and Da told you it was from a pork chop."

They all started laughing. Kiernan and his brothers had teased Cam for weeks about that adventure, but their mother had shushed them all, insisting that Cam should do whatever he dreamed of doing.

"Listen, I have to get home and pack," Kieran said. "I'm the first off. You guys don't leave until tomorrow." He looked at the envelope of cash they'd each been given for the trip. "Are you guys going to take some extra money?"

"Grandda said we had to stick with what he gave us," Cam said. "I figure we ought to play by the rules, don't you?"

"Yeah, but I've got an extra day on the bus," Ronan said.

"You know what it is," Cam said. "He came to this country with a hundred dollars in his pocket. I think he wants us to experience what that was like. It forces us to be creative."

Ronan cursed softly. "The old man is nuts. A hundred dollars went a lot further fifty years ago."

"I suppose we'll just have to use our wits rather than our wallets," Kieran said. "We're all smart lads. I'm sure we can figure something out. And he did give us the credit card in case of an emergency."

"What constitutes an emergency?" Dermot asked.

"Imminent death?" Ronan said. "Starvation? The pressing need for a shower and a shave?" He shook his head. "Three and a half days on a bus."

Kieran got to his feet. "I need a ride home."

"Why don't we all go out?" Cam suggested. "We can have a beer and give Kieran a decent send-off. We won't be seeing each other for six weeks. I think a drink or two is in order."

"O'Leary's?" Ronan asked.

"O'Leary's it is," Kieran said.

THE BUS HAD pulled into the station in Denver at precisely 6:45 a.m. Kieran glanced down at his watch through bleary eyes. His layover was just a little longer than two hours and he wasn't sure he could keep his eyes open long enough to make his transfer onto the next bus headed to Indianapolis.

After his first restless night on the way east from Seattle, he had actually been grateful to change buses in Missoula and Billings, using the opportunity to stretch his legs. But the trip was starting to wear a little thin now and he found himself getting crankier by the mile.

Over the past twenty-four hours, Kieran had managed to read both the books he'd brought with him. He'd tried to check his emails on his BlackBerry, only his grandfather had disconnected his internet access. And the scenery was only interesting when it changed, which happened every hour or so during the daylight hours.

With only a hundred dollars in his pocket, his budget didn't allow for new reading material, so he'd picked up leftover magazines and newspapers from his fellow passengers. He'd read a two-month-old *Sports Illustrated* and a current issue of *InStyle* from cover to cover before finding a copy of some silly tabloid with an alien baby on the cover.

Kieran glanced around at his surroundings. The station was bustling with travelers making their way onto morning buses. He grabbed his bag and walked over to the digital display to check on his departure time and noticed that his bus would start boarding in thirty minutes.

His stomach growled and Kieran reached into his pocket and withdrew his wallet. After careful budgeting, he still had about seventy dollars left as well as the credit card.

They'd been charged with finding a different life and living it for the next six weeks. So far, Kieran had been bored out of his mind with this new life. Though the bus ride had given him time to think about his future, he hadn't really found himself drawn to anything different. He liked his job. It was predictable and interesting and provided a decent living.

Whatever was waiting for him in Bitney, Kentucky would never match what he had in Seattle. Kieran adjusted his bag on his shoulder and headed to the food court at the far end of the station. He found a sandwich shop and ordered a turkey sub and a large Coke.

What he really could use was his usual breakfast

of orange juice, oatmeal and an egg-white omelet. Everything seemed off without his routine.

The cashier totaled up his purchases and glanced up at him. "Ten-thirty," she said.

Kieran frowned. "For a sandwich and a Coke?"

The girl shrugged. "I don't set the prices. Ten-thirty."

He reached into this pocket and grabbed the credit card, then handed it to her. Though it wasn't an emergency, he didn't want to waste any more of his cash. A few seconds later, she handed it back to him. "It was refused," she said in a bored voice.

"No, that can't be. It's a company card. Try it again."

She sighed dramatically and ran it through again. "Nope. Still refused. Do you have cash?"

Kieran looked at the sandwich and soda. At this rate, he wouldn't have enough to feed himself until he got to Bitney. He could wait until breakfast. "Never mind," he muttered.

"I'll get it," a soft voice said.

Kieran looked at the person standing behind him in line. There wasn't much he could see. She wore a baggy sweatshirt with the hood pulled up over her hair. Dark sunglasses hid her eyes. But when he glanced at her hands, he saw perfectly manicured nails and long, slender fingers clutching an armful of junk food. "That's not necessary," he said. "I have cash. I'm just not as hungry as I thought."

"No, take it," she replied. "I insist." When he refused, she sighed impatiently and gathered up his purchases then ordered a soda for herself, before giving the cashier two twenties. "That should cover it. Keep the change."

She turned and handed him the sandwich and Coke. "Thanks," Kieran said. "I can pay you back."

"No problem."

"No, I mean it. I have the cash." He followed after her and when she sat down in the lobby, he took a spot nearby, setting the sandwich and soda between them.

He watched as she unwrapped one of her candy bars and took a bite. She chewed thoughtfully, then shook her head, setting it aside. "Those used to taste so much better." She ripped open a bag of BBQ potato chips and plucked one out. "I haven't had these in years."

She held out the bag and he shook his head. "No, thanks."

"Eat your sandwich," she said.

Kieran picked it up and started unwrapping it. "So, are you some kind of health-food nut?" he teased as she picked through the purchases on her lap.

"What?"

"Breakfast of champions," he said, pointing to the pile of candy.

She shook her head. "I can never decide what to eat. I usually just get anything that strikes my fancy and then nibble through it until I find something satisfying."

"That's kind of a waste of money, don't you think?"

She held out a candy bar. "You can have this. I don't know why I bought it."

"You don't want it?" he asked, taking it from her.

"No, I've already lost interest. Oh, peanut butter. That sounds really good." She opened the candy bar and took a bite, then wrinkled her nose. "Nope, that's not it either." She wrapped the candy up and handed it to him. "I don't have any communicable diseases. Don't worry."

Kieran took a bite of his sandwich, not quite believing this stranger. "So, where are you headed?"

"Don't know yet. I haven't bought a ticket. I thought I would think about it while I ate."

"With all that sugar, you won't need a ticket. You'll be able to run wherever you want to go."

She giggled. "Very funny. Where are you going?"

"Bitney, Kentucky," he said.

"Kentucky? Really? That's where I was thinking about going. I love Kentucky. My grandparents live there."

Kieran watched her suspiciously. Who was this woman? And why had she chosen to entertain him with her presence? Could he really believe her story? "What's your name?"

"What's yours?" she asked.

"Kieran," he said. "Kieran Quinn."

"Hmm. Strange name." She held out her hand, the fingertips stained with melted chocolate. Noticing, she wiped her hand on her sweatshirt. "Maddie. I'm Maddie." She paused. "Maddie Smith."

He took her hand in his and the moment they touched, Kieran felt an odd sensation race through his body. "Nice to meet you," he murmured, "Maddie Smith."

He grabbed his sandwich and took another bite. She had a beautiful voice, strangely melodic with just a tinge of whiskey rasp in it. Though he couldn't see her eyes, her mouth more than made up for that. It was a perfect Cupid's bow, lush and kissable, stained a deep berry color. He imagined that she'd taste of cherries if he kissed her.

A strand of hair teased at her temple—a warm blond color, like honey. Well, she was intriguing, that much he'd give her. But after twenty-four hours on a bus, almost anyone with a personality would be intriguing.

"I noticed that you were a little short of money," she said. "I was wondering if you'd like to make a little more?"

"How?" Kieran asked.

"I need you to go to the counter and buy me a ticket. If you do that, I'll give you a hundred dollars."

He gasped. "Just to buy a ticket? Why don't you want to buy your own ticket?"

"Because I need to get out of town without being

noticed," she explained. "And I'm not sure if they're going to ask me for I.D."

"Hmm. You've done your best to hide your appearance, you want to get out of town unnoticed and you have a lot of cash. Please don't tell me you pulled a bank job."

She laughed a little too loudly, which caused some of the passengers around her to turn and stare. "No. I've been putting aside some cash for a while. And I need to get out of town unnoticed because I'm running away and I don't want anyone to follow me."

"Oh, well, that makes much more sense. How old are you?"

"A gentleman never asks a lady that," she said.

"Take off your glasses and let me see your face," he said. "I'm not going to be responsible for helping some teenager escape a silly fight with her parents."

She took off her sunglasses and tipped her chin up. "I'm twenty-four," she said.

His breath caught in his throat as his gaze took in the details of her face. She was no teenager. She looked to be in her mid-twenties, exactly as she claimed. Her eyes, a beautiful caramel color, were ringed with dark lashes, but he only caught a quick glimpse before she put the sunglasses back on.

Why anyone so beautiful would hide behind dark glasses and a baggy hooded sweatshirt was beyond him. He found himself mentally undressing her, slowly discovering the treasure beneath.

"Satisfied?" she asked.

"Not entirely," he said, swallowing hard.

Maddie reached into the pocket of her hoodie and withdrew a handful of crumpled cash. "Here. Just go get a ticket."

"To where?"

"Kentucky."

"Where in Kentucky?"

"Same place you're going, I suppose," she said.

"Hey, I don't even know what's in Bitney. It could be an awful place to—"

She gave him a gentle shove. "Do it, now. There's no line."

"Okay, okay," he said. "Watch my stuff." Kieran glanced back at the woman as he walked to the ticket counter. This was turning into some trip.

He gave the agent the necessary information and watched as the man typed it into the computer. A few seconds later the agent handed Kieran a ticket. "That will be $196.00," he said.

Kieran peeled off enough cash from the wad Maddie had handed him, then grabbed the ticket. "Thanks," he murmured.

By the time he got back to her, she'd created a small pile of discarded candy bars on his seat. "Licorice," she said. "I could really go for some red licorice right now."

He handed her the ticket and her change. "How about putting something other than sugar into your system?" He tore his sub sandwich in half and offered it to her. But her attention was drawn to the wide entrance doors.

She quickly stood, pulling the hood closer to her face. "Save me a spot on the bus," she muttered. "And don't let them leave without me."

"Where are you going?"

"Licorice," she said.

With that, Kieran watched as she hurried off toward the back of the station. Then he looked around and noticed two men surveying the people seated in the lobby. They split up and slowly walked through the crowd. Kieran didn't like the look of them. They were wearing dark glasses and were dressed all in black, their sport jackets straining against their broad shoulders and massive arms. They looked like the kind of guys hired to guard the door at a nightclub—or commit a felony.

As one of the goons walked by, he noticed all the candy on the chair next to Kieran. He stopped and Kieran looked up at him.

"You like candy?" the guy asked, pointing to the chair.

"Sure," Kieran said.

"Is that yours?"

"Yeah. I kind of have a sweet tooth."

The man reached in the breast pocket of his blazer and pulled out a picture, holding it out in front of Kieran. "You see this girl around here? If you have, it might be worth a little money."

Kieran took the picture and studied it shrewdly.

He'd been right about her. She was gorgeous. "Who is she?"

"Have you seen her?"

Kieran shook his head. "Nope. I would definitely have noticed a girl like that."

The goon tucked the photo back into his pocket, then moved on. Kieran watched him. Had anyone else seen Maddie sitting next to him? They'd all turned to look at her when she'd laughed, but would they connect that girl to the scruffy-looking person in the torn jeans and hoodie?

Kieran cursed softly. There wasn't much he could do for her now. He had no idea where she was hiding and if he got up and left, the guy in the suit might be suspicious enough to follow. Though every instinct warned him that she was in trouble, for some strange reason, he wanted her to make it onto that bus. After all, she still owed him a hundred dollars.

She should have known her mother would send Nick and Rick after her. What she hadn't expected, though, was that they'd start at the bus station. Why not the airport?

Oh, yeah, it would be easy to trace her movements at the airport. That's why. And she didn't have a driver's license so a car was out of the question. The only way for her to get out of town without leaving a paper trail was by bus. Maybe she should have found a hotel room and holed up for a few days. Then again, she'd have to register and show I.D. "The train," she muttered. "I should have tried the train."

Of course her mother could never allow her just the slightest bit of freedom. God, she'd been under her mother's thumb for years, doing exactly what was expected of her. But after this tour, she'd had enough. Now that she'd sung her last show on the calendar, she was going to start living her life in the way she wanted.

Maddie West, award-winning country singer-songwriter, had been transformed from a talented teenager into a multi-national corporation in the course of ten years. A multinational corporation who couldn't get up onstage without a double dose of Xanax and a few hours of hypnotherapy.

But the drugs weren't working anymore. And the hypnotist her mother had hired for this tour was sleeping with her make-up artist and no longer cared about solving Maddie's problems. No one really cared about her needs anymore. Making money was all that mattered and touring was where all the money was made.

Maddie pulled her knees up to her chin and sighed softly. Maybe she ought to go back. There were a lot of people depending on her. And she was scheduled to head into the recording studio next week to start her new album. They'd booked the time with her favorite producers and there were meetings scheduled with her record company in Nashville.

She closed her eyes, brushing aside her doubts.

A single image lingered in her mind. What was his name? Kieran. Kieran Quinn. Such an odd name. And yet, it suited him. From the moment she spied him at the food court, she sensed that he'd be sympathetic to her cause. He had very kind eyes—and a face that made a girl want to tear off all her clothes and find the nearest bedroom.

A shiver skittered down her spine. How long had it been since she'd felt that kind of chemistry? Maddie's love life had always been the stuff of tabloid stories and never, ever lived up to the hype. She'd dated a few actors, a few singers, a smorgasbord of up-and-coming males who looked good on paper, but didn't excite her in or out of the bedroom. But lately, she'd grown cynical about ever finding love, especially amid the pressures that the press exerted on romantic relationships.

"My life is a mess," she murmured. There wasn't one single element that she could point to as normal. Her mother was overbearing and unrelenting, running her career and her personal life as if Maddie were some prize racehorse. She was carefully groomed and trained, watched over twenty-four hours a day, told what to eat and when to sleep, when to practice and how to relax. Maddie wasn't even sure she knew how to run her own life, given the chance.

A sliver of fear shot through her. What if she couldn't do it? What if she finally made her escape and couldn't exist on her own? She drew a ragged breath. For now, she had a protector. And maybe, she could convince him to stick around until she figured out her next move.

Maddie pulled her cell phone from her pocket. She'd shut it off when she'd snuck out of the hotel, but now she wondered whether they could track her using it. She glanced around the luggage room, wondering if she ought to leave it behind. Was that how Rick and Nick had found her?

As she weighed her options, Maddie heard the announcement for her bus. If she tried boarding too early, she'd be caught standing in line, a sitting duck for her two shrewd bodyguards. But if she waited too long, she might miss the bus entirely. Maddie took a deep breath. She'd just keep her head down and keep walking, no matter what happened.

She slipped out of the door and headed back into the waiting room of the terminal. "You can do this," she murmured. "Just a few more minutes and you'll be free."

"Where have you been?"

She felt Kieran's hand on her arm before she realized he was behind her. "Go away," she whispered.

"They're outside," he said. "They're watching everyone who boards the buses, but that's a lot of people to watch. If you're careful, you should be able to get by them."

She stopped. "I can't let them take me back. You have to help me."

Kieran considered her, then nodded. "All right.

Wait right here. I'm going to see if I can distract them. As soon as I do, you sneak out and get on the bus. Just make sure you get on the right bus. And save me a seat."

"Thank you," she murmured. She reached into her pocket and withdrew another wad of money. "Here, take this."

"How much cash do you keep in your pockets?" he asked.

"I don't know. A couple thousand, maybe three."

"Don't go flashing that around," Kieran warned, pushing her hand back in her pocket. "You're going to get mugged." He shook his head. "Just get on the bus."

Maddie nodded. She watched him through the window as he strode outside. When he approached Nick, she held her breath. Between Nick and Rick, Nick was the smart one. He was naturally suspicious and very loyal to her mother. What was Kieran going to tell him? And what would she do if one of them stayed and watched the buses?

A few seconds later, the two men took off running, racing through the doors of the terminal, right by her. She waited until they headed toward the ticket counter, then slipped through the doors. She walked directly to her bus, handed the driver her ticket and got on. Maddie found a seat halfway to the back and slipped into it, sinking down and watching the activity outside the window through her dark glasses.

Kieran had disappeared. When the bus driver

stepped onto the bus and reached out to close the door, Maddie stood up, ready to shout for him to stop and wait. But then, at the last moment, Kieran came bounding up the steps.

He handed his ticket to the driver, then made his way down the aisle to Maddie. With a grin he nodded at the space next to her. "Is this seat taken?"

"I was kind of saving it," she said. "But you can sit here. For now."

Kieran stowed his bag on the overhead rack, then dropped down next to her. As the bus pulled out of the station, Maddie closed her eyes and sighed deeply.

"And the adventure begins," Kieran murmured.

"Thank you," Maddie said. "I couldn't have gotten away without you."

"Are you going to tell me what you're running away from?" he asked.

"Can we just wait on that one?" she said. "I'd really like to enjoy anonymity for just a little bit longer."

Kieran nodded slowly. "All right. But there is one thing you have to do for me."

"What's that?"

He reached out and gently removed her sunglasses. Folding them neatly, he tucked them into his jacket pocket. Then, he pushed the hood from her head, his palms smoothing across her face. Maddie closed her eyes and turned into his touch.

It was such a simple gesture, but in an instant,

she felt a flood of warmth rush over her. When she opened her eyes, he was watching her, his gaze fixed on her mouth. Maddie waited, wondering what was going through his head. Kissing him would complicate everything, but then, it could also make a boring bus trip much more interesting.

"Why did you help me? You don't even know me," Maddie asked.

"I don't know. I guess I figured there was no one else who was going to ride to your rescue."

"No one ever does anything for me without some kind of motive."

"Well, you did give me money, and I'm broke. So, I guess I did it for a sandwich and the half-eaten candy bars. And I was hoping for some fascinating company on the rest of my trip."

He really was a nice guy, Maddie thought to herself. And he was sexy as hell, too. She'd made so many bad choices when it came to men… Then again, she'd never dated an ordinary guy.

Maybe that was her problem. When she slept with celebrities, there were so many expectations to live up to. They were supposed to be heroic and larger-than-life and she was supposed to be the ultimate bad girl.

But she'd always been disappointed. Her lovers were never as strong and gallant as she imagined. And she was never as uninhibited as they'd undoubtedly imagined.

It was difficult to allow herself any type of freedom when the end result might be splashed all over the covers of the tabloids a few days later. She'd lived her life paralyzed about what the press would say, always suspicious of strangers and wary of friends.

It had been simple for her mother to maintain control. After all, she was the only one that Maddie could truly trust. But lately, Maddie had begun to notice that her mother had motives of her own. More money, more fame, more of everything that she'd come to enjoy. And when Maddie had mentioned that she might want to give up performing and just focus on songwriting, her mother's true feelings had burst forth.

Why couldn't she have had a normal life? A childhood filled with friends and school, a world where there was still so much opportunity laid out in front of her. Maddie felt as if she'd already lived a lifetime. She felt old and tired, cynical and unhappy with life.

"I guess I owe you," she said softly, brushing aside the urge to kiss him. Maddie reached into her pocket and counted out one hundred dollars. "Here. This is for buying the ticket."

He shook his head. "That's all right. You hang on to it. I know where to find you if I need it."

"I'm really tired," she said with a soft sigh.

Kieran patted his shoulder. "Here, you can lean up against me. Close your eyes and take a nap. We've got a long ride ahead of us."

"You're a really nice guy," she murmured as she wrapped her arms around his. Pressing her cheek to his sleeve, she drew in a long breath. "You smell good, too."

Kieran chuckled. "I wouldn't breathe in too deeply. I've been on a bus for twenty-four hours. I could use a long, hot shower and some clean clothes."

"Me, too," she said. "A shower would be perfect." Maddie closed her eyes and let her thoughts drift. But they didn't wander back to the life she'd run out on, her mother's angry face or her manager's warnings that her career would be over if she didn't perform. Instead, they focused on the man who had rescued her from certain discovery.

It sure was nice to have someone in her corner for once.

2

FOR THE FIRST time since he'd boarded the bus in Seattle, Kieran slept. Not just a half-conscious, restless nap interrupted by the slightest noise or jolt. He was out, completely unaware of his surroundings, lost in a deep, satisfying slumber.

Afterward, he and Maddie chatted, learning a little bit more about each other as the Kansas landscape passed by. Chatted, he thought to himself. That was a benign word for what they'd done. Full-on flirting was a more apt description. They'd laughed and teased, injecting tiny sexual innuendos into the conversation at every turn.

And when the teasing wasn't enough, there had been the casual, almost accidental physical contact. A touch here and there, her warm hand on his arm or his face, his shoulder bumping against hers.

When they'd grown bored with silly stories, they'd found a discarded book of crossword puzzles in the overhead bin and had filled in the empty spots on the half-finished puzzles, arguing over the answers playfully.

It was the most fun he'd had with a woman in— well, ever. He could be himself with her, not afraid to reveal the flaws he kept secret from others.

She found his obsession with financial matters charming and his constant checking of the schedule strange. She'd called him a "stuffypants" and a "human calculator," not to mention a few other things that he might have taken as insults coming from anyone else. But Kieran liked that she spoke her mind.

And yet, they hadn't talked about anything serious, or anything real. He still didn't know the circumstances that brought her to the bus station or why she felt the need to run. All she'd said was that the life she'd left had become too much for her.

The lunch stop had been at a small diner along the interstate and once again, Maddie had ordered four or five entrees from the menu, then picked through them until she found something that piqued her interest—this time a grilled cheese sandwich and a strawberry shake. Kieran hadn't even bothered to order. He simply enjoyed the dishes she rejected. He was getting to know her faults as well, and didn't mind them a bit.

They pulled into Topeka at a quarter after eight in the evening, fifteen minutes earlier than scheduled. He thought about getting out for something to drink, but Maddie was dozing beside him, her arms wrapped around his, her cheek resting on his shoulder.

As he stretched his other arm over his head, he noticed two young girls standing in the aisle staring at him. "Hi, there," he murmured.

They giggled and pointed to Maddie. "Is that Maddie West?" they asked.

Kieran frowned. He should have suspected his Maddie was using an alias. "Who is Maddie West?" he whispered.

"The country singer," one of the girls said. "Can we have her autograph?"

"This isn't Maddie West," he said calmly. "Sorry. She gets that all the time. Her name is Alice. Alice Smith. But I'll tell her you thought she was Maddie West. She'll get a kick out of it."

The girls walked down the aisle and out of the bus, disappointed. Kieran looked at the woman sleeping beside him. So she was Maddie West, country singer? Now, suddenly, the reason she'd had the two goons looking for her made perfect sense. They were probably her bodyguards. And for all he knew, they believed she'd been abducted. Maybe it was about time for some answers.

Kieran turned and shook her gently. "Maddie," he whispered. "Maddie, wake up." She groaned softly. "Maddie, they need you onstage."

Maddie's eyes flew open and she jolted upright, scrambling to pull her hood over her tousled hair. "What? Now?" Rubbing her eyes, she looked around the bus, then groaned. "What are you doing? Why would you do that to me?"

"I think maybe it's time for you to tell me the truth. The whole story."

"There is no story."

"Then maybe I should tell those little girls out there that they can come back and get Maddie West's autograph. Because they seemed pretty damned impressed that they were on the same bus as a big country-music star."

With a low curse, she sank down in her seat. "Oh, great. There's nowhere I can go in this world to get away from it. It follows me everywhere."

"Not everywhere. I didn't recognize you. But then, I'm really not a fan."

"I figured that out right away. It was one of your most endearing qualities." She quickly stood. "I have to get out of here. If those girls recognized me, then it won't be long until everyone on the bus is looking at me."

"Where are you going to go?"

"I don't know. Where are my sunglasses?" He handed them to her and she put them back on her nose, then pulled her hood over her hair. "I can't stay here." Maddie held out her hand. "Thanks for everything. I really appreciate you riding to my rescue." When he refused to shake her hand, she turned to hurry down the aisle, then paused.

A moment later, she stumbled back to him and threw her arms around his neck. Her lips met his, soft and sweet and unbelievably exciting. Kieran slipped his hands around her waist and pulled her closer. The kiss was so unexpected and yet so perfect.

Her lips parted and Kieran took the invitation to explore more deeply. A tiny moan slipped from her throat as their tongues met and his hands slipped beneath the sweatshirt, circling a tiny waist and pulling her down into his lap.

He'd known this girl, this woman, for a half day and yet, they seemed to sense what the other wanted from the kiss. Kieran settled her against his body, furrowing his fingers through her hair. The high backs of the seats hid them from the view of the passengers still on the bus and they lost themselves in a rare moment of privacy.

When she finally drew back, she sent him a winsome smile. "I hate goodbyes," she said.

"Me, too."

"I really should go. I have to keep moving or they're going to catch up to me."

"Why are you running? That's a little drastic, don't you think?"

"I just want a different life for myself and this is the easiest way. I don't want to argue anymore or fight, I just want to wake up each day and feel as if it's going to be the best day of my life, not the worst." She paused. "Maybe you could come with me?"

The offer was so tempting. But Kieran had other responsibilities to fulfill. He'd made a promise to his grandfather and no matter how beautiful she was and how much he enjoyed kissing her, he was bound for Bitney, Kentucky. "I can't. I have to go to Kentucky."

"I still want to go to Kentucky," she said. "We'll just find a different way. Maybe we could go by train?"

"I don't have the money for a ticket," he said.

"If you come with me, I'll buy your ticket. And your meals. It'll be fun. I've never taken a trip on a train. Don't you want a little adventure in your life, Kieran Quinn?"

Kieran groaned inwardly. If he went with Maddie, life would certainly become a lot more interesting. And who knew where things might lead between them.

He'd always been so careful about how he lived his life, especially when it came to women. But his grandfather had wanted him to imagine a completely different life for himself. Taking a cross-country road trip with a runaway music star would certainly be something new.

"All right," he said. "But how do we know that we can catch a train here?" He shook his head. "I don't know where we are."

"Topeka," she said. Maddie pointed out the bus window. "And there's a sign for the Amtrak station right there."

"Then let's go." He grabbed her waist and set her in the aisle, then stood up and got his bag from the overhead rack.

"Really? You want to come with me?"

"Yeah, I'm looking for a new life, too. I don't think it matters if I start the search in Topeka, Kansas, or Bitney, Kentucky, as long as I find it."

Maddie held out her hand. "All right. Let's go."

They hurried off the bus, Maddie's identity once again obscured by the hood and the sunglasses. Kieran wasn't sure what the future held with this crazy, impulsive, sugar-addicted woman, but hitting the road with Maddie West was sure to be much more fun than another five hours on a bus.

When they stepped onto the platform, there was a crowd gathered nearby. Suddenly, one of the girls who'd asked for an autograph jumped out from the crush of people. "There she is! That's her. That's Maddie West."

Kieran was shocked at how fast the people surged toward them both. And he was doubly shocked at how quickly he reacted. He grabbed Maddie's hand and pulled her around to the other side of the bus. "We need to go. Right now."

Luckily, there was a cab parked on the street about fifty yards away. If they could reach it before the crowd got to them, they'd be safe.

With a scream, Maddie took off, pulling him along behind her. She was quick and nimble, crossing the distance like an Olympic athlete. She quickly crawled in the backseat of the taxi, ordering the driver to go as Kieran threw his bag in the backseat. He got inside as the cab was pulling away from the curb, then looked at Maddie. She was smiling, her color high, her pretty green eyes flashing.

"Where to?" the cabbie asked.

"I don't know," Maddie said. "Just drive for now. We'll figure it out later."

Kieran, breathless from the run, grinned at her. And then, adrenaline took over. He grabbed her and pulled her into a long, desperate kiss. His hands frantically grasped at her clothes, wanting to touch her anywhere, everywhere at once. And Maddie was just was frantic, her fingers working at the buttons of his shirts.

When they finally drew back, they were both still breathless. The cab driver watched them in the rearview mirror. "Are you someone famous?" he asked.

Maddie laughed. "No. Not anymore."

"You know, I once had Willie Nelson in my cab. He was a real nice guy."

"I'm sure he was. Could you take us to the Amtrak station?" Kieran asked.

The train station was only a few blocks away. Kieran decided to have Maddie wait in the cab while he checked the schedule. Unfortunately the next train east wouldn't leave until the following morning at 5:00 a.m. He bought two tickets with the money Maddie had given him, upgrading to a private room to keep fans from recognizing her.

When he returned to the car, she was waiting. "The next train leaves tomorrow morning," he said.

"What are we going to do?"

"I suggest we get a hotel, take a shower, relax and get a decent night's sleep."

"Take us to a nice hotel, please," Maddie told the cab driver.

"Nice but cheap," Kieran added.

"No, not cheap," Maddie said. "We want room service. And a big bathtub would be nice. And maybe someplace nearby where I could buy some clothes."

"Everything downtown is closed," the cab driver said. "I could take you out to the Target. It's just a couple miles north of here. They're open twenty-four hours and their prices are real reasonable."

"There we go," Kieran said. "Reasonable."

"Why are you so hung up on money?" Maddie asked. "We have plenty." She turned to the cab driver. "All right. Target, first, then a nice hotel near the station. Something with room service."

"I'll fix you up," the cabbie said. "No worries."

They both sat back in the seat. "You know, we really should be more careful with your money. You're not even sure how much you have," he whispered.

"You seem to be more worried about my money than I am." She grabbed the cash out of her pocket and handed it to him. "Here, you take care of it. There's more where that came from."

"If you use a cash machine, they might be able to trace your movements."

"I have a secret account," Maddie said. "No one knows about it, not even my mother. And I have this debit card." She pulled a card out of her pocket. "So, stop worrying about money, Mr. Scrooge. I've got it covered."

Being too free with money went against every instinct he had, but he wasn't living his own life anymore. Why not see where this led him? It might be fun to stop worrying about every move and be more like Maddie—spontaneous and impulsive.

"All right. You're in charge."

Maddie reached out and gave him a hug. "See? We'll make wonderful traveling companions."

In truth, Kieran wasn't so sure. It was easy to keep his hands off of Maddie when they were out in public, riding on a bus or sitting in the station. But sharing a hotel room for the night was tempting fate. Though getting two rooms wasn't budget-conscious, it would certainly would delay the inevitable.

Kieran knew he and Maddie would end up in bed together. And whether that happened tonight or further on down the road, they wouldn't be able to avoid it very much longer.

MADDIE STARED AT the selection of hair coloring, trying to decide. In the end, she pulled seven boxes of color in various shades of auburn, blond and brunette and tossed them into her basket. She'd figure it all out later.

Since she'd decided to start a whole new life, she figured the best way to do that would be to leave everything behind, including her five-hundred dol-

lar hair color. No more celebrity stylists, no more designer gowns and red-carpet appearances. She could
finally live the life she wanted.

Maddie couldn't imagine what this trip would be
like if she'd been alone. Maybe she wasn't cut out
to live her own life. She'd never had the chance to
try. Most girls graduated from high school and went
off to college, breaking away from their parents and
learning the skills needed to get along.

She'd never had her own apartment, never paid a
bill or made an appointment for herself. Everything
had always been done by her business managers or
her mother. And she'd missed out on so much—high
school dances and football games, graduation and
the first day of college.

The only problem was, Maddie wasn't quite sure
what this new life of hers should look like. When
she imagined her future, it was only a blurry image,
without any detail. All of her dreams had revolved
around a singing career. But now, the only thing that
she could really see in that image was a man.

Kieran was exactly what she'd always dreamed of.
He was handsome and sexy and kind. And better yet,
he hadn't had a clue who she was when they first met.
And here they were, like two normal people, strolling
through Target late at night, shopping for…stuff.

"Hey."

Maddie turned to find Kieran standing next to
her. "Hey."

"What are you looking at?"

"Nothing," she said, turning away from the hair color.

He grabbed a box from the basket. "You're going to color your hair?"

Maddie shrugged. "Maybe I won't get recognized so easily. I'm going to cut it, too." She glanced over at him. "So, what do you think? Redhead or brunette?"

Kieran frowned. "I kind of like it the way it is. The color and style suits you."

"It's not real," she murmured, staring at a strand. "Besides, I need a fresh start." She pulled the boxes out of the basket and set them back on the shelf, leaving only a light brunette. "This is close to my natural color. That should do."

He held out a CD to her. "Look what I found," he said.

Maddie stared at the cover of her second CD, then took it from his hand. "This was a good album. I remember when I made this. I was sixteen."

Kieran wrapped his arms around her waist. "You look so young."

"I was so young. Just a kid. I thought this was what I wanted to do for the rest of my life, the concert tours and the awards shows. But it was a trap. Once it sucks you in, you can't escape. Unless some guy forces you to buy him a turkey sandwich and then just won't go away."

"But you were good at it," Kieran said. "You must have been."

She sighed and handed the CD back to him. "You

should never achieve your dreams so early in life. There should be a rule against it."

"If you don't go back to singing, what are you going to do?" he asked.

Maddie shrugged. "I don't have to do anything. I have plenty to live on for years. And I can always write more songs. I like doing that."

"You must be good. There's a whole bin of your CDs in this store."

"I am good," she said with a smile.

"Do you have everything you want?"

In truth, she had everything she needed. She had a sweet and impossibly sexy man to occupy her thoughts and soothe her doubts. He kept her grounded, gave her sensible advice and watched over her. And when he touched her, her body tingled and her knees went weak.

"I need to get a few more things," she said. "Some underwear. And shoes."

"I can help you with the underwear," Kieran said, grinning.

Her thoughts moved to what was going to happen later that night. Once they got a room, there wouldn't be much to do except explore the attraction between them. Sure, she could order dinner and maybe watch a movie, but it was silly to pretend that they didn't want to spend their time in other pursuits.

A shiver skittered down her spine as she thought about all the possibilities. Suddenly, she realized that there was a purchase she still had to make. Condoms. But putting them in the cart might add too much pressure. She just wanted to be prepared, just in case. "Why don't you go check out the underwear and I'll join you there," she suggested. "I—I'm just going to—run to the bathroom." She pushed up on her toes and kissed his cheek.

Maddie hurried away, but as soon as she saw him head down another aisle, she returned to the health and beauty section. Only when she reached the condoms, Maddie was faced with another dilemma—too much choice. Did she want large or extra large? And what about color, ribbed or lubed?

She grabbed three boxes and hurried to the cashier. But when she got there, she realized that she'd given all her cash to Kieran. Maddie pulled out her debit card and walked up to a checker, dumping the boxes on the conveyor belt.

The checker gave her an odd look. Maddie smiled. "Big night," she murmured. Thank God, she was still wearing her sunglasses. She could imagine the tabloid stories if anyone recognized her. *Country star starved for sex? Maddie West, sex addict? Maddie the Nymphomaniac?* The debit card had her real name on it, Sarah M. Westerfield, so that offered a bit of safety.

"Credit or debit?" she asked.

"What? Sure. Whatever. Debit."

The cashier finished checking Maddie out and then put the three boxes in a small bag. Maddie stuffed them into her pocket, then smiled as she took her receipt. "I've got more shopping to do," she said, then walked back into the store.

Maddie found Kieran where she'd sent him, in the underwear section. He was leaning over the shopping cart, studying the selection of bras. When he saw her approaching, he straightened and smiled.

"People were starting to wonder about me," he said. "I think they thought I was some kind of pervert."

"I guess that remains to be seen," she said, grinning. "So, what have you picked out for me?"

"Well, I've always been partial to black. And I think lace is pretty." He paused. "Should I really be picking out your underwear?"

"It's nice to have a male opinion," she said.

"Am I going to be seeing your underwear?" he asked.

"It's a distinct possibility," she said. "Do you want to see my underwear?"

Kieran chuckled. "I wouldn't mind taking a peek. I bet they're really pretty." He drew a sharp breath. "Can we just quit talking about it and buy some?"

Maddie tossed her choices into the cart, then mentally went through her shopping list. Shampoo, hair color, scissors, mascara, hair dryer, underwear, a few cute outfits, three cotton dresses and—"Luggage," she said. "I need a bag to put all this in. And shoes."

But as they walked to the shoe department, Maddie caught sight of a rack of party dresses. A couple of teenage girls were going through them, giggling excitedly as they held their choices up in front of them.

"I bet they're going to a dance," Maddie said. "I've never been to high school dance."

"Neither have I," Kieran said.

"You didn't go to prom?"

He shook his head. "I wasn't actually very smooth with the girls. And I didn't get too involved in school. My brothers and I spent most of our free time together, working on our boats or sailing. Girls just weren't very important back then." He paused. "Of course, that all changed in college."

"I never went to college, either," Maddie said. She looked back toward the girls. "You know, I think I need one of those dresses. Every girl needs a party dress."

"Where are you going to wear it?"

"I don't know. Maybe on the train?" She pressed her finger to his lips. "And don't tell me I shouldn't waste my money."

"I wasn't going to do that," Kieran said. "I actually think a party dress might be exactly what you need."

With a giggle, Maddie turned over control of the cart to him and walked over to the rack. "I'm just going to try a few on."

As she looked through the dresses, the two teenage girls gave her an odd look. In truth, Maddie could understand their curiosity. She was still wearing the hoodie and her sunglasses. They whispered to each other, watching her from behind a nearby rack.

"It's for my niece," Maddie said to them, grabbing a pink taffeta strapless gown with a huge tulle skirt.

The girls approached. "Are you—"

"You're going to say Maddie West, aren't you," Maddie quickly replied. "I get that all the time. Do you really think I look like her?"

"She gets that all the time," Kieran confirmed, nodding his head.

Maddie put the pink dress in the cart, then quickly grabbed a slinky black number from the end of the rack. "All the time," she said, pushing the cart away.

They hurried though the shoe department, the girls following them at a safe distance, their curiosity piqued. When they reached the checkout, Maddie tugged her hood down over her forehead.

"Would you mind paying for all this while I wait out in the cab," she murmured. At his nod, she walked out of the store.

When Maddie reached the safety of the taxi, she jumped into the backseat. The cabbie was reading a magazine. He glanced up at her in the rearview mirror, then twisted in his seat. "Are we waiting for your friend?" he asked.

"Yes," Maddie said. "Of course."

He nodded. "No problem."

Maddie thought he'd turn around again, but instead, he stretched his arm across the back of the front seat. "If you don't mind me asking, what's a famous singing star like you doing running around a big box store in Topeka, Kansas?"

Maddie moaned and covered her face. "You, too?"

He nodded. "I saw you on the CMAs last year. You were just great. You're the most famous person I've ever had in my cab. I mean, you blow Willie Nelson away."

"What's your name?" Maddie asked.

"Ron. Ronald. Ronald J. Widmer."

"Listen, Ronald. Do you think you can keep my secret? There'll be a really big tip in it for you. And if you'll give me your address, I'll send you a complete collection of my CDs when I get home. And I'll sign them all. Do you think you could do that for me?"

He gasped. "I'm sure I could. I always thought being a star has to be a hard life. I just want you to know, you have a friend in me. Ronald J. Widmer."

Maddie smiled. "Thanks. I really appreciate it. And—and don't believe any of the stuff you read in the tabloids. None of it is true."

"Oh, I know that." He held up the tabloid he'd been reading. "I just like them for the Bigfoot stories."

Maddie smiled to herself. If things didn't work out with Kieran, she always had Ronald. "Thanks, Ronald," she said. "I really appreciate your discretion. Sometimes, it's nice to just be anonymous."

"But sometimes, it sure must be nice to be famous," he said with a chuckle. "I wouldn't mind tryin' that out for a day or two."

MADDIE SAT IN the center of the bed in a nest of pink tulle. She'd found a small bottle of champagne in the minibar and was sipping bubbly out of a coffee mug from the room-service tray.

Kieran watched her from the sofa. They'd both grabbed a quick shower while they were waiting for their room-service dinner to arrive.

Her long hair, still damp from her shower, curled around her face in pretty tendrils. Even from across the room, the scent of her was intoxicating. With any other woman, he wouldn't have thought twice about seduction. And he had to admit, thoughts of seducing Maddie had been running through his mind from the moment he'd met her.

But there was something that had stopped him— or at least slowed his pace toward the inevitable. Though she seemed tough and resilient on the outside, he sensed that it was all for show. She was a scared and vulnerable woman, trying to find her true path in the world. And he wasn't about to take advantage of that. Not until they were both ready.

She dribbled champagne on the front of her frock and brushed it off with her fingers.

"Why are you wearing that dress?" Kieran asked.

Maddie shrugged. "Oh, I don't know. I just wanted to celebrate. I feel like I've been let out of prison." She paused. "You know, sometimes I wish I could go back and live the last ten years all over again."

"What would you do differently?" Kieran asked.

"I'd stand up to my mother," she said. "And I'd

keep my song-writing talents to myself until I turned eighteen. It's true what they say about child stars. We are all screwed up."

"You're not screwed up," Kieran said, pushing to his feet and crossing the room to stand beside the bed. He held out his hand and when she placed her fingers in his palm, he pulled her up to her feet. She stood on the bed in front of him and Kieran slipped his hands around her slender waist.

"You look very pretty."

"I think I actually believe you," she said.

"And why wouldn't you?"

"Because people tell me exactly what I want to hear all the time. After a while, I don't really know what to believe or who to trust."

He nuzzled her belly. "You can trust me, Maddie. I'll always be honest with you."

"I know I can," she murmured. Her fingers furrowed through his hair and she tipped his face up until he met her gaze again. "So, you really think I look pretty?"

He nodded.

"Then why haven't you kissed me again?"

"Do you think I kiss every pretty girl I see?" he asked. "Why haven't you kissed me?"

"I don't know. I've been thinking about it a lot. But now that we're all alone with this big bed, I thought kissing you might start something we might not be able to stop."

"And we barely know each other," he said. He

lifted her off the bed, drawing her into his embrace. "I can stop. Just say the word."

He bent close and found her lips, soft and slightly parted. This time, he took it slowly, savoring every sensation and sweet taste of her. Before, the kisses they shared were like excited outbursts, but this time, he meant to seduce her. After this kiss, she'd know exactly what to expect if she didn't tell him to stop.

Her hands smoothed over his chest, then slipped up to circle his neck. She felt so perfect in his arms, her slender body finally revealed from beneath the baggy hoodie and faded jeans.

Though Kieran had enjoyed his share of no-strings lovers, he didn't consider Maddie one. There was something special about her. With her, it wouldn't be just an exquisite physical release. They'd somehow forged an emotional connection, starting that morning in the Denver bus station. He'd become her protector and he didn't want to do anything to hurt her.

Maddie pulled him down on the bed and he stretched out on top of her, bracing his weight with his hands on either side of her, their mouths still joined. This was all so new to him, Kieran thought. Usually a night in bed came with certain expectations. But he didn't know what would happen here.

"I don't want you to stop," she whispered.

His breath caught in his throat. The invitation couldn't have been any clearer. But it wasn't quite right. They still felt a little bit like strangers, and though the desire was obvious and intense, neither one of them seemed ready to cast aside all their inhibitions. How would they feel in the morning? Would they regret what they'd done?

He drew back, his lips hovering over hers. God, it took every ounce of his willpower to stop himself, but he was determined that he wouldn't give in to his impulses. "We should probably get some sleep," he murmured. "We've got to get up and be at the station in about eight hours."

"Or we could stay up the rest of the night and sleep on the train," she said. "I'm finally free. I want to celebrate."

"You don't have to do it all on your first day," he said. "Come on. Why don't you put on something comfortable, then we'll crawl under the covers and turn off the lights."

"Can we keep kissing?" Maddie asked.

"I don't think I could stop."

She turned around, then glanced over her shoulder. "Unzip me?"

Kieran groaned inwardly. If she planned to sleep in the nude, he'd be lost. There was no way he could resist a naked body next to him. With fumbling fingers, he did as she asked, then grabbed a T-shirt from his bag. "Here, you can wear this."

She hadn't bothered to put on underwear beneath the pink party dress and as it dropped to the floor, he caught a tempting sight of her naked backside. She stepped out of the dress as she pulled the shirt over her head, then turned to face him.

Kieran pulled the covers back and she crawled into the bed. "I'm just going to pull out the studio couch and sleep there," he said.

"No," Maddie countered, sliding across to the other side. "It's a king-size bed. There's plenty of room for both of us. Don't worry. I'll behave."

"I'm not worried about you," Kieran said.

"And I'm not worried about you," she said.

Kieran reluctantly sat down on the edge of the bed and pulled off his shoes, then swung his feet up onto the mattress.

"You're going to wear your clothes to bed?" she asked.

"I think that might be best." He reached over to turn off the lights. When the room was dark, he felt Maddie's body shift next to him. A moment later, she was curled up against him, her hand resting on his chest.

He wondered if she could feel his heart pounding, could sense his nerves fired in anticipation. Though he wasn't hard, it wouldn't take more than a simple caress to get his blood pumping in that direction.

Kieran slipped his arm beneath her head and pulled her closer. She began to hum softly, a tune he didn't recognize. But it was sweet and relaxing and he closed his eyes and pressed a kiss to the top of her head. He felt her relax against him and after a time, her humming stopped and her breathing grew soft and even.

She was such a complicated creature, he thought

to himself. To an outside observer, she had the perfect life—an amazing career, people all over the country who loved her, a talent that very few possessed, and an inner strength that he found quite attractive. And yet, she longed for something simpler.

They did share one thing. Neither one of them were living their dreams. The more time he spent with her, the more Kieran realized that he'd never really thought much about what he wanted. He'd accepted his responsibilities with the family business and was happy to go along as he had been—doing his job, enjoying his free time sailing.

But what were his dreams? He'd always thought about spending a year sailing down the West Coast and up the East Coast, traveling through the Panama Canal. He wanted to learn how to surf. And he wanted to feel the kind of excitement he felt when he was with Maddie every day of his life.

Was she his dream? Kieran drew a deep breath, then slowly let it out. He'd never thought much about committing himself to just one woman. Marriage and family seemed such a long way off. But he was twenty-seven years old. It was time he decided what he really wanted out of life.

He glanced over at the clock beside the bed. They had to get up in four hours if they were going to catch their train. Kieran reached out to set the alarm, then decided that there was no need. He wouldn't get any sleep tonight, not with Maddie curled up next to him.

Kieran pulled her closer, wrapping his arm around

her waist. He'd expected this trip to be an exercise in boredom, but it had become the exact opposite. With every minute he spent with her, he felt himself changing.

He liked not knowing what tomorrow held, not having a carefully constructed plan. For all he knew, tomorrow might be the most amazing day of his entire life—or a total disaster. But that didn't matter. If he was with Maddie, then it would always be a good day.

3

MADDIE OPENED HER eyes to see the early-morning sun pouring through the hotel window. This time, she knew exactly where she was. She didn't have to think about it or reach out for her itinerary. She was in bed, with Kieran Quinn, in Topeka, Kansas.

But one question came quickly to mind. What time was it? Weren't they supposed to get up to get on a train at five in the morning? She pushed up on her elbow and wiped the sleep from her eyes, then peered at the bedside clock. It was 9:00 a.m. The train had left about three hours ago.

Maddie groaned and flopped back down into the pillows. Knowing Kieran's penchant for schedules, he was not going to be pleased. And if the tickets weren't refundable, he'd have something to say about that, as well. But then, if she made the prospect of an extra day in a hotel room more interesting, he might not complain.

He'd be happy if she had breakfast waiting for

him when he woke up. Maddie slipped out of bed and fetched the menu from the nearby desk. She tiptoed into the bathroom and closed the door, then stared at herself in the mirror.

Her hair, still damp when she'd fallen asleep, was a riot of curls, falling in tendrils around her face. She grabbed the toothbrush she'd bought last night and brushed her teeth, then picked up the phone next to the toilet.

She ordered strawberry waffles, eggs Benedict, a Denver omelet, a basket of pastries, orange juice and a big pot of coffee. At the last minute, she added a side of grits and biscuits with gravy.

Drawing a deep breath, she smiled to herself. Spending an extra day in Topeka wasn't in the plan, but she felt safe here. It would be nice to have some time to just relax with Kieran.

Maddie wandered back out into the bedroom. She picked up her cell phone from the desk and looked at it. She knew there would be multiple messages from her mother waiting in her voice mail and in her text box. A tiny twinge of guilt worried at her and she fought the temptation to call her mother and let her know that she was all right.

But if her calls and texts could be traced, she didn't want to risk it. Her mother was relentless and would do and say anything to drag her back. Maddie just needed a few more days. Then she'd be able to deal with her mother in a more calm and rational manner.

Maddie set the phone down and crawled back into bed, curling against Kieran's body. Her fingers toyed with the front of his shirt, stretched tight across his chest. He looked so sexy while he slept, his hair rumpled, his lips parted slightly and his arm thrown over his head.

Turning, she pressed a kiss to his neck. When he stirred, Maddie moved to his ear. He opened his eyes and looked at her, then frowning, he glanced over at the clock.

"We missed our train," he said, his voice low and raspy.

"We did," Maddie said, kissing his chin.

"I didn't set the alarm. I didn't think I would fall sleep."

She brushed her lips across his. "You were definitely sleeping. You were even snoring."

"I don't snore," he said.

Maddie kissed him again. "Just a little bit."

"Well, you talk in your sleep," he countered. "You carry on entire conversations with yourself. Last night it was something about a green dress and ear muffs and a blue purse."

Maddie giggled. "I told you I was a little crazy. I've also been known to sleepwalk when I'm under stress. Once I was in San Diego on tour and I walked out into the hall of my hotel and locked myself out of my suite. My mother was still inside, so she let me back in. Which was a lucky thing, because I was stark naked." She paused. "You don't mind that we missed our train, do you?"

He looked at her for a long moment, then smiled. "No. I guess an extra day in this hotel isn't going to kill us."

Maddie crawled on top of him, stretching her body out over the length of his. He groaned softly as the friction of their hips teased at his morning erection. "I wouldn't be so sure of that," she teased. "You've never spent a day in bed with me."

"And just what do you have planned?" he asked, his hands smoothing over her waist to rest on her naked backside.

Maddie reached for the buttons of his shirt and slowly undid them, one by one. "I think maybe we should get you out of this shirt." With every inch of chest she exposed, Maddie kissed his warm skin. A soft dusting of hair ran from his collarbone to a spot beneath the waistband of his jeans.

He had the most incredible body, Maddie mused as she skimmed her palms over his chest. He was slender, yet muscular, the body of a man who enjoyed physical activity but probably never set foot in a gym. He was a real man, not one of those strange celebrity hybrids who merely looked like the ideal.

"Are you sure you want to do this?" he asked.

"I don't know," she replied. "What are we going to do?"

"Mess around?"

"Don't you want to?" she asked.

He reached up and ran his fingers through her hair, pulling her close to meet his gaze. "Maddie, there's nothing I want to do more then spend the day making love to you. Let's get that clear right off the bat. But I don't want you to think that I'm expecting it or that it's not going to mean anything."

"You're getting all serious on me," she said. "I thought we were having fun."

"I don't want to be just one of those candy bars you buy. After you get a taste, you toss me aside and move on."

Maddie frowned. "What exactly do you expect from me?"

"I want you to consider the fact that once we do this, it might change everything. We might just discover that there's something more to this than we imagined."

"I might want to eat the entire candy bar?"

He chuckled. "I don't know. Maybe."

Maddie shook her head. "There you go again. You constantly overthink things. You need to learn to stop worrying and just react."

She ran her hand down his belly, dipping beneath the waistband of his jeans before retreating. "How does that feel?"

"Tempting," he said.

She bent over and kissed his nipple, her tongue lingering for a long moment. "How about that?"

"That's very nice," he said.

"Now, you try it." She watched as he drew his

hand along her hip before gently cupping her breast in his palm. Maddie closed her eyes as delicious sensations coursed through her body. He brought her nipple to a hard peak, rubbing gently with his thumb through the soft fabric of the T-shirt.

"What were you thinking?" she asked.

He grabbed her waist and rolled her over, then slowly tugged the T-shirt up to reveal her belly. He pressed his mouth to her warm skin, moving higher until he found her breast. Slowly, he teased her with his tongue. Maddie felt every nerve in her body come alive. Desire surged through her veins like a river of fire.

"I was thinking you might just be the most beautiful woman I've ever touched."

A soft rap sounded at the door and Maddie sighed. "I ordered breakfast. Could you eat? Because I'm really hungry." She crawled off the bed and headed to the door, pulling his T-shirt down over her backside.

Kieran sat up in bed and watched as the waiter rolled the cart into the room and handed Maddie the check. She quickly signed it and gave it back to him, then shut the door after he stepped into the hall.

The cart was loaded down with food and she pushed it over to the bed, then poured him a cup of coffee. "I love this," she said.

"Breakfast?"

"No, breakfast with you. It's such a nice way to start the day."

Maddie set the plates of food in the center of the

bed, then removed the covers, revealing her choices for breakfast. She dragged her finger through the hollandaise sauce from the eggs Benedict and put it in her mouth. "Umm, that's going to be good."

"What am I going to eat?" he teased.

Maddie plucked a fresh strawberry off the plate of waffles and held it out for him. "Stop complaining."

He dug into the Denver omelet, setting the plate on his lap and balancing the coffee cup on a nearby pillow. "So, what's the plan for today? I'd really like to get out and take a walk if the weather is decent. I feel like I've spent the last week sitting on my ass."

"I kind of thought we could spend the day in bed," she said.

"Breakfast, walk, then back to bed," he said.

"All right. But before we go out again, you have to help me do my hair."

"I know nothing about hair." He reached out and slipped his fingers through the curls around her face. "Are you sure you want to cut this?"

Maddie nodded her head. "Sorry. But I'm ready for a change."

"Me, too," he said.

"What are you going to do?"

"I don't know. Maybe I should get a tattoo. Or I could get my ear pierced."

"I could pierce your ear. I just need a needle and some alcohol." She pulled one of the diamond studs out of her ear. "You could wear this. And after we pierce your ear, we can do our nails and talk about boys." Maddie clapped. "We are going to have fun."

With a low growl, he pulled her down next to him and grabbed her forkful of eggs Benedict. He popped it in his mouth. "That does taste good," he murmured.

"Maybe I should order a pitcher of hollandaise sauce and pour it all over my naked body."

"Now, that would be fun," Kieran said. "And a completely new culinary experience for me."

THE WEATHER IN Topeka was stifling, hot and humid. Dark clouds rumbled in the distance and it looked like the afternoon would be punctuated with storms. They walked out of the hotel into a blast of warm air and Kieran was almost tempted to turn them both around and return to the air-conditioned comfort of their room.

But it felt so good to get out and move around. He slipped his arm around Maddie's waist and pulled her close. They managed to do her hair, coloring it a slightly darker tone and cutting it off at the shoulder. If it was possible, she looked more beautiful than she had before. The wavy strands tumbled around her face in a way that made it look like she'd just crawled out of bed. She wore her sunglasses and between the hair and the glasses and the discount-store dress, she definitely looked different from the rumpled runaway he'd met in the bus station the other morning, not to mention the glamorous star on the covers of her CDs.

There wasn't a lot to see around the hotel, but they started down the wide boulevard, toward a cluster of stores and restaurants, holding hands and strolling without any purpose.

"I should have bought a swimming suit last night," she said. "The hotel has a pool." She looked up at the sky. "I was supposed to go into the recording studio next week to start my new album." A sigh slipped from her lips. "It looks like it's going to rain."

Kieran glanced over at her, wondering at the series of disconnected comments. She had something on her mind, but obviously wasn't ready to talk to him about it, so she was dancing around the subject.

"What's wrong? You look worried."

Her shoulders rose in a shrug. "I almost called my mother this morning before you woke up. I was feeling guilty. She's probably worried and we've never gone this long without speaking to each other. But I'm afraid to call her—I don't want her to figure out where I am. I just need a little more time."

"A little more time? You sound like you're thinking about going back."

She ran her fingers through her hair, pressing the heels of her hands into her temples. "Oh, I don't know," she cried. "There are so many people that count on me. If I don't work, then they don't work. The thing is, if I make this new album, then I have to go out on tour to promote it. You can't make an album without touring. So if I'm going to quit, this is the time."

He studied her shrewdly, smoothing a windblown strand of hair from her eyes. "Do you really hate singing that much? You're obviously really good at it, Maddie. You couldn't have sold all those albums if you're not good."

"I do love to sing. But not to such huge audiences. And with the band and all the lights and craziness. There are so many ways things can go wrong and there's so much pressure to be perfect. Do you know how much people pay for tickets? So, of course they expect a perfect show." She grabbed his hand and wove her fingers through his. "And if I'm not perfect, the press won't leave it alone. So many people are depending on me for—"

Kieran stopped her rant with a kiss, his lips soft on hers. "I understand."

Maddie smiled. "I believe you're the first person who does."

They found a coffee shop close by and Maddie ordered a frozen mocha before they continued their walk to a small strip mall. She stopped in front of a pawnshop window and peered inside, still sipping on her coffee.

"See anything interesting?"

"Let's go in," Maddie said. "I want to look at that guitar."

Kieran opened the door for her and they stepped inside the cool interior. The place was filled, floor to ceiling, with items for sale. Maddie pulled the guitar from the window display and carefully examined it while Kieran wandered over to the electronics.

As she talked to the elderly salesman, Kieran watched her, admiring her slender body and beautiful features. If she thought that cutting her hair would make her less noticeable, she was completely wrong. She was still stunning. In truth, every time he looked at her, he found something new that he liked.

He turned back to the electronics and peered into a glass case at a portable GPS. He had one just like it at home but he could use another to put on his boat as a back up. And this was a decent price. Unfortunately, he didn't have more than seventy dollars to his name.

Kieran chuckled to himself. He had barely seventy dollars and it didn't bother him in the least. He wasn't worried about money or time or even getting to Bitney, Kentucky. That would happen when it happened.

"Can I show you anything?" the salesman asked, appearing behind the counter.

"Yeah, I'd like to look at that GPS."

The salesman took it out of the case and Kieran examined it.

"What is that?"

He turned to find Maddie standing next to him. He handed it to her. "It's a global positioning system."

A frown furrowed her brow. "I have no idea what that is."

"It tells you exactly where you are in the world. Latitude and longitude. Right down to a few feet either way."

"Does it tell you where you're going to be tomorrow or the next day?" she asked.

Kieran chuckled. "No. It doesn't predict the future."

"Then what good is it? I know where I am now. I'm in Topeka, Kansas."

"It's a good thing to have in case you get lost and you need to find your way back home."

Maddie slipped her arms around his. "Maybe we do need it."

"Or maybe it's good to get lost once in a while," Kieran countered. "What kind of adventure is this if you always know where you're going?"

Kieran handed the GPS back to the salesman. "Thanks, but I'm going to pass on it," he said with an apologetic shrug. "Are you going to buy anything?" he asked Maddie.

"I'm going to take the Martin guitar," Maddie said, nodding. "It has a case, right?"

"A hard-shell case. It's in decent condition."

"Good. I'll give you five hundred for both."

The salesman thought about the offer for a long moment, then nodded. "Deal." Maddie turned to Kieran and wiggled her fingers. "Cash, please."

"I thought you were giving up music," Kieran said.

"And I thought it would be nice to have on the train. I can teach you how to play."

Kieran held up his hands. "Oh, no. I have absolutely no musical talent. Beyond singing in the car with the radio, I'm pretty much a hopeless case."

"A lot of people start out that way," she said. "I happen to be a very good teacher."

"If you teach me how to play the guitar, what am I supposed to teach you?"

She thought about it, then smiled. "You can teach me how to drive," she said.

"We don't have a car."

"We'll figure that out. We could always rent one. A convertible. I've always wanted one of those old Cadillac's with the tail fins. You know, a classic sixties car."

Kieran looked around. "They don't have any cars here," he said.

"Actually we do deal with cars, as well," the salesman said. "There's a lot out back. I could show you a few if you like."

"No, no, no," Kieran said. "We're taking the train."

"We're taking the train," Maddie said, nodding in agreement.

They paid for the guitar and walked back out into the midafternoon heat. Kieran took the guitar from her hand. "I'm going to be your roadie," he said.

"If you were my roadie, I would have broken one of the cardinal rules of touring."

"And what is that?"

"Don't sleep with the roadies," she said, laughing. "You never would have gotten past my mother. She approves all hiring on tours. She would have known that you'd be too tempting to resist, so you never would have gotten the job." She paused. "It's funny, but we probably would have never met if we hadn't run into each other at that bus station. I might have decided to fly. Or your bus could have arrived late. And yet all the fates conspired to—"

"What?"

"I'm going to write a song about that," she said. "I have to go back to the hotel now."

"You don't want to get some lunch?"

Maddie shook her head. "No. You get something to eat. I really want to get this idea down before it slips out of my mind."

"I'll walk you back," Kieran said. He took her hand as they hurried down the sidewalk, startled by the sudden change in her. He'd just assumed Maddie was always playful and a little flighty. But now, she seemed so completely focused that he had a hard time adjusting to the change.

Kieran wondered if he'd ever really know her completely. Maybe that was a good thing. There was always something new to discover, something interesting to learn about this beautiful woman. And he wanted to know it all.

"A TOAST," KIERAN SAID, holding up his champagne flute. "To your new song. Whenever I hear it, I'm going to think of Topeka. And the two nights I spent with you."

Maddie giggled, the effects of a half bottle of champagne bubbling up inside her. She sent Kieran a sexy gaze. "I left my heart," she sang, "in Topeka, Nebraska."

"Kansas!" Kieran said. "We're in Kansas."

"Whatever," Maddie said. "Nebraska, Kansas. I'm just happy I'm here."

They'd enjoyed an early dinner at the hotel restaurant. Maddie felt a bit guilty after she'd spent the afternoon, alone in their room, working on a new song. But when inspiration struck she knew enough to take advantage of it. It rarely came with such strength and focus as it had that afternoon. Though she wanted to leave her professional world behind her, at least for a time, she would have to make a living sooner or later. And she never knew where the next hit song would come from.

"Maybe sometime you'll sing it for me?" Kieran asked, watching her over the rim of his champagne flute.

"Maybe," Maddie said. She wasn't sure why she wasn't ready to sing for him yet. Maybe she just wanted to leave her professional life behind a little while longer. Or maybe, she was afraid if she did sing, he'd take her mother's side in all matters and urge her to get back onstage.

Now that the song was written and committed to memory, she'd decided to turn her full attention back to Kieran. She put on her party dress, fixed her hair and invited him to join her in the hotel restaurant.

"That dress suits you," he said.

"Thank you." Maddie slipped out of her shoe and ran her foot along his thigh beneath the table.

His eyes went wide. "What are you doing?"

"I'm trying to seduce you. I've gotten you drunk and now I'm moving on to step two—overt physical contact. But I'm obviously not doing a very good job if you can't figure that out."

"Sweetheart, you don't need to try. Just looking at you across the table is enough to get me going."

"It's the pink dress, isn't it?" she said, brushing the tiny strap off her shoulder.

"No. I'd want you even if you were wearing that hoodie and your beat-up jeans. It wouldn't make a difference."

"You know, I'm not wearing anything under this dress."

Kieran groaned. "Don't tell me that. I was really looking forward to ordering dessert. They have banana crème pie."

Maddie took another sip of her champagne, then reached for the bottle to refill her glass. But the bottle was empty. "Do you want to order another?"

Kieran shook his head.

"Are we going to do this?" she asked.

He nodded.

She set her champagne flute down, then stood up and tossed her napkin on the table. "I'll race you.

First one to the room gets to undress the other." With a laugh, she took off through the restaurant. Maddie looked back over her shoulder to see him dealing with their waiter and the check.

She made it to the elevator first, but as she was waiting, he caught up to her. To her surprise, he headed for the stairwell. They were on the seventh floor and she knew she'd never beat him up the stairs.

Maddie punched at the button and a moment later, the elevator doors opened. She hurried inside and pressed the button for her floor, but as the doors were closing, an elderly couple hurried toward her.

"Hold the elevator," the man called.

She glanced over to the panel, cursing softly, then stepped forward and caught the door. The couple smiled gratefully as they got inside and pressed the button for the third floor. The doors closed and the elevator moved upward.

When she finally reached the seventh floor, Maddie stepped out of the elevator and walked to the room. Kieran was waiting at the door with the key card, his shoulder braced against the wall, his arms crossed over his chest. He wasn't even out of breath.

"You win," she said.

"Oh, don't look so disappointed," he teased. He unlocked the door and held it open. "We're both about to get naked and do what we've been waiting to do since the moment we met."

She arched her brow, giving him an inquisitive

look as she passed. "Since we met? You were thinking about this in the bus station?"

"Well, not this. But I was attracted and thoughts of a sexual nature did cross my mind. I remember thinking that your lips would probably taste like cherries. I'm a guy. What can I say?"

He followed her into the room, then grabbed the Do Not Disturb sign from the door and hung it outside. Maddie waited for him, the champagne making her mind buzz and her body boneless. He sat down on the end of the bed and slipped his hands around her waist, pulling her toward him.

For a long moment, he didn't move. He just stared up into her eyes. Had he changed his mind? Was he going to find some excuse not to ravish her? Maddie knew the attraction between them was mutual. So why was it taking him so long to make a move?

But then he slowly turned her around and reached for the zipper of her dress. After it was down, he brushed the skinny straps off her shoulders. The dress slipped off her body and puddled at her feet in a pile of rustling tulle.

Maddie felt his hands on her body, smoothing over her shoulders, then moving down to her hips. She closed her eyes as he pressed a kiss into the small of her back.

She'd always been careful about her sexual relationships in the past, never completely trusting the man she was with. But now, for the first time, Maddie felt as if she could truly enjoy herself. Kieran had no ulterior motives. They were just two normal people who had met in a bus station.

She slowly turned. Though he was still completely dressed and she wasn't, she didn't feel a trace of inhibition. Maddie watched as his gaze skimmed her body. When he looked up at her again, she smiled. "Excuse me for a moment," she murmured.

Maddie walked to the closet and found the condoms that she'd purchased in the pocket of her hoodie. Clutching the bag in her fingers, she returned to the bed and held it out to him.

"What's this?"

"Necessities," she said. She turned the bag over and the three boxes of condoms fell onto the bed. "I wasn't sure what kind you liked, so I bought a variety."

He chuckled softly. "Thank you. For thinking of me."

"I wasn't sure that you'd—you know…"

"I always keep a box in my shaving kit, but these are very interesting…options."

Maddie reached out and took his hands, pulling him to his feet. Her fingers dropped to the buttons on his shirt and she worked them open, then smoothed the soft cotton fabric from his shoulders.

His body was so perfect, so beautiful. Broad shoulders, a finely muscled chest, sinewy arms…it was all as it should be—undeniably masculine. His jeans came next and by the time she slipped them over his hips, he was already hard, his erection pressing against the front of his boxers.

Maddie took his hand and brought it to her breast. She smiled as he touched her, his thumb teasing at the growing peak of her nipple. And when she leaned forward and their lips met, she knew what he'd known all along. This was meant to happen.

It was crazy, so thrilling and a bit frightening, these feelings whirling around inside her. She'd never felt such raw desire before. The attraction between them was powerful and the need for intimacy so strong that it ached inside her.

"I think you should pick a condom," she said.

"It can wait," Kieran replied. "We have plenty of time."

She slowly shook her head. "I don't want to wait. I'm not a big fan of foreplay."

"Sweetheart, then you haven't been with the right man." He grabbed her hips and pulled her beneath him, then slowly kissed his way from her lips to her neck to her breasts.

Maddie slipped her fingers through his hair as she arched against him. She didn't care if this was both the first and the last time they made love. But she knew it was going to be the best she'd ever had.

When he reached her belly, Kieran slid off the bed and pulled her to the edge. Gently, he parted her legs and placed a kiss on her inner thigh. She moaned softly and he kissed her other thigh, gradually working his way up to the damp spot between her legs.

When he ran his tongue along her slit, Maddie felt a current race through her, setting every nerve in her body on fire. Her fingers twisted in his hair, at first pushing him away, then drawing him closer.

It was obvious Kieran knew exactly how to pleasure a woman. He'd no doubt managed to satisfy a long string of beautiful women with this particular talent. But she didn't feel an ounce of jealousy or envy. He was hers now and she wasn't about to give him up.

Maddie felt the climax building inside her, teasing at her senses until every thought was focused on the feel of his mouth on her body. She arched against him and delicious shivers coursed through her body. So close.

She held him back one last time, trying to regain her composure. But by now, the orgasm was just a heartbeat away. When his tongue touched her again, her body tensed, then shattered into a series of deep and powerful spasms.

He continued to tease her, drawing out her release until it seemed that she couldn't move. Every ounce of her self-control had dissolved until she was weak and spent. When he rejoined her on the bed, stretching out beside her, Maddie was smiling.

"I think I might have been wrong about foreplay."

4

KIERAN GROANED SOFTLY as Maddie crawled on top of him. "We have to get up in two hours."

She straddled his hips, rocking back until he had a perfect view of her naked body. He wasn't sure he'd ever get enough of looking at her. There was still so much they didn't know about each other, so many pleasures yet to enjoy. Missing the train again wouldn't be the worst disaster in the world.

"I think we should just stay up. You know, remain active."

"We've been active since you dragged me into bed," he said, pulling her down into a long, lingering kiss. "I burned off that dessert I didn't have for dinner."

"Oh, I know how hard it is." She giggled as she rubbed against him. "Or how hard it's quickly becoming. But, don't you think you could rise just once more to the occasion? We can always sleep on the train."

"We're not going to sleep on the train if we miss it. I couldn't figure out how to switch our reservations, so I had to buy two new tickets. I'm not wasting any more of your money missing another train. Besides, anything we can do here we can do on the train."

Maddie drew her finger along his bottom lip. "As much as public sex might be a personal fantasy of yours, I'm not going to do it on a train. I was brought up better than that."

"I got us a room," he said with a grin. "It's really nice. It has a bed and a bathroom and lots of privacy. I figured you wanting to remain incognito and all, we should probably spend the extra money."

"Good idea. As my transportation coordinator, you're doing a very good job. I think maybe I ought to be giving you a bonus." She shifted against him. "A really...nice...bonus."

"Whatever you say, boss." His hands spanned her waist. "But I want you to promise me something."

"What's that?"

"You're not going to hire any more employees. I'm not sure I'd like to share my bonuses." With a growl, he pulled her down beside him and threw his leg over hers.

"Bossing you around is about all I can handle," she murmured. "Now, are you going to take care of my needs, or will I have to take care of yours?"

"I'm the one getting the bonus, not you."

Maddie reached for the box of condoms on the bedside, pulling one out and tearing it open. She smoothed the condom over his stiff shaft. Just the touch of her fingers was enough to push him closer to the edge. "I think this is much better than a few extra dollars in my paycheck," he said, his voice low.

Maddie pulled him on top of her. "You don't get a paycheck," she replied.

Kieran nuzzled her neck as she drew her legs up alongside his hips. He already knew the incredible feeling of burying himself deep inside her and he'd come to crave it as much as the feel of her flesh beneath his fingers or the taste of her mouth.

What quirk of destiny or fate had put this woman in his path? When he'd stepped on the bus in Seattle, he was sure that nothing worthwhile was waiting for him in Bitney. He was sure that his grandfather's plan was just an exercise in futility.

But then Maddie had just stumbled into his life and changed everything. Was this all part of some grand cosmic plan? Or was it just pure chance that had brought them together?

As he slowly buried himself inside of her, he couldn't deny the power of their sexual attraction. But there was so much more between them. For the first time in his life, he'd found a woman who was completely open and honest with him.

In the past, he'd always sensed he wasn't getting the whole story, that even in bed, women were just pretending to be who they thought he wanted them to be. But this was real. It felt right to be with Maddie.

Drawing a deep breath, he closed his eyes, enjoying the sensation of their bodies so intimately joined. And when he began to move, Kieran knew there would never be another woman like her.

She reached up and ran her fingers through his hair, drawing him into a passionate kiss. With every stroke, he felt the connection between them growing stronger.

Kieran grabbed her thighs, then gently pulled her on top of him, the weight of her body driving him more deeply inside her. He watched as she moved, her lithe body open to his touch.

At first, her pace was slow and languid. But when he reached between them, to tease at her need, her expression grew focused. She stared down at him, a tiny smile curving the corners of her mouth. The closer she came to her release, the more he found his own pleasure increase.

Kieran wanted to feel that moment when she lost control, but it was more and more difficult to deny his own body. Every cell seemed to be alive, vibrating together until there was no other choice but to surrender.

But then, as if she knew what he was waiting for, Maddie gasped, pressing her hands into his chest, her body tensing. A moment later, she gave him what he'd wanted all along, dissolving into breathless shudders. Kieran followed her, his orgasm deep and powerful, wringing the last bit of desire from his body.

Maddie collapsed on his chest, her hair tickling

his face. Kieran closed his eyes and drew in the scent of her shampoo, smiling to himself. "We are never going to get out of this hotel room," he murmured.

"Would that be so bad?"

"I guess not. But we're going to run out of money sooner or later."

"No, we won't. We have plenty. I've still got a lot of cash left as well as my debit card. There's lots of money in my account."

"Aren't you worried that your mother could trace the card?"

Maddie sat up, her hair tumbling around her face. "She doesn't know about it. It's my runaway money. I've been saving it for the past two or three years."

"You've been planning to run away for that long?"

Maddie nodded. "I had to open a bank account. I couldn't hide any more cash under the lining in my guitar case. I get a per diem when I'm on tour and I just saved it all. My mother never noticed that I wasn't spending anything. I also get my royalty checks, but I send that money to my grandparents."

"You said they lived near Bitney."

Maddie nodded. "I haven't seen them in such a long time. I'm glad we're going there. They have a horse farm. You'll like it. I used to spend summers there when I was a kid."

"When I was young, I was fascinated with horses. My ma used to buy me little figurines and we'd play with them. I had palominos and pintos and dappled grays. And I had books and movies. *My Friend Flicka* was my favorite."

"And you never learned to ride?"

"I had big dreams of being a cowboy. But after my mom died, I just kind of lost interest."

"She died when you were young?" Maddie asked.

"You don't want to hear my sad story," he said.

"I do. You know all of mine. Well, maybe not all of them. But you know a few. How did your mom die?"

"She and my dad were sailing a boat to the South Pacific and they just disappeared. We never heard from them again."

A gasp slipped from her lips and her eyes went wide. "Just like that? They were gone?"

Kieran nodded. "I was nine. We moved out of our house and went to live with my grandfather."

"You were an orphan? Why haven't you told me this?"

"I guess it just didn't come up."

"It should have," Maddie said. She shook her head. "I feel awful."

"It happened a long time ago," Kieran said.

"No—I mean, I do feel awful for you. But this whole time, I've been going on and on about how horrible my mother is and how I could hardly wait to get away from her and—and—"

Her eyes filled with tears and she brushed them aside. Kieran sat up, alarmed by the sudden turn in her emotions. "Oh, don't cry. It's all right. It was a long time ago. And your relationship with your—"

"I'm selfish," Maddie snapped. "I think everything revolves around me. I never even thought to ask about you and your family. I mean, you told me about your brothers, but I just assumed everything had been—happy. You seem so normal, I thought you'd had a normal life." This brought another flood of tears.

"Don't cry," he said, brushing his lips against hers.

"How horrible for you. I feel so bad."

"Maddie, we've known each other for three days. Not even that long. I figured we'd get to that story sooner or later. Sometimes, it's just difficult to explain. And people usually react like you. Which makes things even more difficult."

Forcing a smile, she brushed her tears away. "Sorry. It's just so sad." She wrapped her legs around his waist and kissed him again, her backside nestled in his lap. "I didn't have a father, but I never really missed him. He was never part of my life. Your parents were just ripped away."

"We adjusted," Kieran said. "My brothers and I were—and are—really close. And my grandfather did his best. But he really didn't know how to deal with grief like that. We hung out at work with him and learned the business. And that's why I'm here, on my way to Bitney."

"I don't understand."

"My grandfather wanted us all to find a different life for six weeks. Since we didn't have a chance to follow our own dreams, he thought by sending us all out into the world with a bus ticket and a little cash, we'd find out whether we were living the life we wanted or the life we'd been handed."

"You're on a quest," she said.

"Me and my three brothers. Although, I can't imagine that their quests have turned out anything like mine."

"Tell me more about your brothers," she said. "And your childhood. I want to know everything. Even the bad stuff."

Kieran pulled her down beside him, her body stretched out against his. "We'll have time," he whispered. "I'll tell you everything you want to know. But right now, I'd rather kiss you."

They had to get up and get packed in about an hour. And right now, he just wanted to close his eyes, pull her naked body against his, and sleep. Sad stories could wait.

"All right," Maddie said, wiping away the last of her tears. "Next time, I won't cry."

"That would be good," he murmured, kissing her temple.

THEY BOARDED THE train fifteen minutes before departure. The attendant helped them find their room, a tiny cabin with a pull-down bed and a closet-sized bathroom. A bottle of champagne and a basket of fruit sat on the small table between the seats and they were informed that breakfast would be served in the dining car after the train left the station.

But Maddie wasn't interested in food. She had the attendant pull the bed down, then crawled into it. The gentle rocking of the train lulled her into a deep sleep that began outside Topeka and didn't end until the train was somewhere in Iowa.

For Maddie, this was the perfect way to travel. She and Kieran were alone, with everything they needed to be comfortable. They caught up on their sleep and after they got up, Kieran went to the dining car and fetched their lunch, a tasty sandwich with fresh fruit and French fries.

They continued their conversation about his childhood and hers. He opened up about the fears and confusion during the time of his parents' disappearance, the grieving that never seemed to come, and the effect it had had on him and his brothers. And she tried to comprehend how a boy so young could handle such a tragedy.

As the rural landscape sped by, Maddie curled up beside him on the wide seat, her feet tucked under her, her head resting against his shoulder. They'd found comfort in each other, a mutual understanding that made sense of their childhood troubles. Maddie couldn't imagine another person in the world who could understand her like Kieran did.

The train pulled into Chicago just after three in the afternoon. They disembarked, then wandered around the old station for a few hours, waiting to board the line that would take them to Cincinnati. From there, it was still another hundred miles to her grandparents' farm, but she wasn't worried. Kieran would find a way to get them where they needed to go.

"I don't want this to end," Maddie said, as they settled themselves into a new cabin for the nine-hour ride.

"Maybe we should just keep going. Where does this train stop?"

"Washington, D.C.," he said. "And then I think it goes on to New York."

"Oh, let's keep going," Maddie said. "I'd love to go to New York. We'd have so much fun."

"I thought you wanted to see your grandparents," he said.

Maddie nodded. "I do. But we can do that later. We only have six weeks before you have to go home. I want to do everything and see everything."

He pulled her down beside him in the seat, settling her on his lap. "We can't keep spending money like this. You're going to have to stop running and face your mother."

"But I've saved for this," she said. "Why can't I just go where I want? It's my life now. And my money."

"I need to find work," he said. "I can't keep sponging off of you."

"You're working for me," Maddie said. "You're

like my bodyguard and tour manager and traveling companion all in one. I can pay you." She drew a deep breath. "All right, let's just get this whole money thing out of the way."

"Money thing?"

"Yes. You always come back to it and I want to put it all out on the table. How much do you need to make? Now, think carefully because I want it to be enough so that we never have to discuss this again. And I don't ever want to hear you whining about how much we're spending. We spend what we spend. End of story."

"I don't need you to pay me."

"But you said you had to find work. And I want you to work for me. For as long as you can." She paused. "Six weeks. How much would that cost?"

"Six weeks?" Kieran said.

Maddie smiled. "All right. Six weeks."

"I have to spend some of that time in Bitney."

"We will. We'll go there after New York."

A knock sounded on their cabin door and Maddie jumped up to open it. The attendant stood outside. "Dinner will be served in an hour. Is there anything I can get you?"

Maddie shook her head. "We're fine. How long before we get to New York?"

"Arrival time is 10:00 p.m. tomorrow night," he said. He turned to leave, then stopped. "By the way, you might be interested in knowing that we have a celebrity on the train. Some country singer named

Maddie West. I don't know who she is, but some of the passengers said they saw her get onboard. If you see her, let me know. They all want an autograph."

Maddie swallowed hard, her spirits falling. "I've never heard of her," she said.

"Well, we don't often have celebrities onboard. They usually fly." He shrugged. "If you need anything, just call. I'll be back to turn down your bed later."

"Thanks," Maddie said. She shut the door behind him, then turned to Kieran. "We have to get off this train."

"Why? There's no reason. We'll just stay in our cabin and get off at Cincinnati, like we planned."

She shook her head. "No. I want to get off at the next stop."

"Maddie, no one has to see you. You'll be fine."

She cursed softly. "You told me you wouldn't argue. That we'd go wherever I wanted to go."

"I know I said that," Kieran countered. "But this is crazy."

"Well, so what. I'm crazy. You knew that from the start so don't act so surprised now. I don't want to be trapped on this train. We'll get off at the next stop and we'll figure out what to do from there."

"You can't run forever," he said.

"I can try."

"I thought you were going to call your mother and let her know you were safe."

"I don't want to talk to her," Maddie said, leaning back against the door. "I know what she's going to say to me. She's going to tell me I have to get back in the studio and work on the next album. And then, she's going to tell me about the tour she's been planning for Japan and Australia. She thinks I don't know about it, but that I won't be able to say no if it's all planned. That's what she does. She makes it so I have no choice. But now, I have a choice and I want to get off this train."

"All right," Kieran said. "We'll get off at the next stop."

Maddie nodded, relieved that he finally agreed. Everything had been so perfect, she didn't want to risk spoiling it all. If he saw—if he knew—what her celebrity life was like, he'd run in the opposite direction as fast as he could.

"How long do we have?"

"I don't know," he said. "I could ask the attendant."

"No. We'll just get off." She sat down next to him. "I'm sorry. I know you should have a say in this, but you don't know what it's like. It's overwhelming. Everyone wants something—an autograph, a photo, a chance to say hello. And I can do that, I love to do it, when I'm in the right mood. But I don't want to do that now. I don't want to smile and be nice. I just want us to have this time alone."

"All right," Kieran said.

He held out his hand and Maddie snuggled against his body. "I'm a bad person," she murmured.

"Yes, you are," he said.

Maddie pushed back, shocked by his glib agreement. Kieran chuckled, then dropped a kiss on her lips. "You pay me to agree with you, Maddie. I'm just doing my job." He paused, then kissed her again, this time lingering over her mouth, his tongue tracing the crease between her lips. "You're not a bad person, Maddie. You're the best person I've ever met. The best."

He always knew exactly what to say to her to make her feel better. "I don't want to seem ungrateful," she said hesitantly. "Because I'm not. These people who buy my CDs and come to my concerts, they're just wonderful. They've made my life what it is. But sometimes, it doesn't feel like it's my life. It feels like theirs. And I get…resentful. And then guilty. And then depressed. It's just one big pile of negative emotions."

"That's understandable," he said. "You deserve to have a life outside your profession. Everyone does."

"You always say the right thing," Maddie said.

"I'm just telling you the truth. Now, don't you think you should call your mother and tell her you're all right?"

Maddie shook her head. "She'll just yell at me and tell me I have to come back. I'll feel guilty and then I'll give in. You don't know my mother. She knows exactly what buttons to push."

"But she is still your mother. She's probably sick with worry."

Maddie knew that contacting her mother would be risky. She'd have to turn on her phone and no doubt there'd be hundreds of texts and messages waiting for her. They saw each other every single day and she still managed to send Maddie ten or twenty texts each day.

"She's like this dark cloud that hangs over me all the time. And I kind of like being out in the sunshine."

"Then get rid of the dark cloud," he said.

She held her BlackBerry out to him. "You do it. That way, I don't have to look at the messages. Just tell her that I'm fine. I'm taking a break and I'll call her next week."

"All right."

Maddie waited as Kieran typed in the text. "Send," he murmured. He glanced up. "Do you want to wait for a reply?"

She shook her head. "No. Just shut it off. I'll deal with it later. Hopefully, she won't send the FBI after us."

Kieran gave her a dubious look. "She'd do that?"

"You don't know my mother. I'm sure she'd try her best to avoid a big scandal. But if it's the only way to get me back, who knows what she'll think of." She drew a deep breath and let it out. "I do feel better now. That dark cloud is gone." She wrapped her arms around his neck and kissed him. "Thank you."

"I'm just here to please," Kieran said with a wicked smile.

"Then you better get to work on that. We don't have much time left and I've never done it on a train."

KIERAN GRABBED MADDIE's hand as they jumped off the train just a few moments before it began to pull away from the station. He glanced around. The station wasn't much, just a small shack not much bigger than a one-car garage. There wasn't even a ticket agent inside. "Well, this is strange," he murmured.

"Where are we?" Maddie asked.

"Dyer, Indiana."

"Maybe we should have waited," she murmured, taking in their surroundings.

"No, it's all right. There's a phone booth over there. We'll find a car rental place and give them a call. They'll bring a car over and we'll be on our way." They walked over to the phone booth only to find that the phone book was missing.

"Do you have internet on your phone?" Kieran asked.

Maddie shook her head. "I could call information."

"It looks like there's a busy street on the other side of the tracks. Let's walk over there and find someplace for dinner and we'll get our plans together. If we find a gas station, we can ask for a phone book there."

Kieran grabbed her bag and hung it over his shoulder along with his, then took her hand. Maddie grabbed her guitar and they started down the long sidewalk next to the tracks. They crossed over when they found a spot leading to the parking lot. To Kieran's relief, they had their choice between a pizza place, a bowling alley and a sports bar.

"Well, what do you think?"

"Definitely bowling," Maddie said with a smile. "I've always wanted to give it a try."

They walked through the parking lot and Kieran opened the front door for her, but Maddie paused. "You take the guitar. Give me my bag."

"Good idea. But if anyone asks me to play, we're going to be in trouble."

The place was busy, but no one seemed to notice their arrival. They walked to the bar and sat down, Kieran dropping the bags and guitar at their feet. He ordered a beer and Maddie asked for a Coke.

She glanced around uneasily, fiddling with her hair and trying to blend in with the surroundings. Kieran took her hand. "What?"

"They're playing my song," she whispered, pointing overhead.

Kieran listened to the tune over the sound system and grinned. He'd never heard her music before but he should have known it was Maddie. It sounded exactly like her. "Wow. That's pretty nice. You're going to have to sing that one for me sometime."

When the bartender returned with their drinks, Kieran paid him, then nodded. "We just got off the train and we need a car. Is there a rental place around here?"

The bartender nodded. "Sure is. There's one out by the airport. Enterprise, I think. And there's another the next town over. I have a buddy who owns a used-car lot there. He also has rental cars if you don't want to go with one of the chains."

"We're going to need a cab, too," Kieran said. "To get to the rental agency."

The bartender chuckled. "Well now, that's a different story. This isn't exactly Chicago, although we're almost considered a suburb these days. But, hey, I'm off work in another hour. If you stick around, maybe bowl a few frames, I can call my buddy and let him know I'm going to bring you around. It's not far. A few miles down the road."

"That would be great," Kieran said. "Thanks."

"Can I get you anything to eat?" he asked.

"Sure," Maddie said. "I could eat."

The bartender stared at her for a long moment, his forehead furrowed into deep lines. "Do I know you?"

Maddie shook her head and quickly took a drink, hiding behind the glass. "I don't think so. This is the first time I've ever been to Dyer."

"Lots of people say she looks like that country singer, Maddie West," Kieran said. Maddie kicked him beneath the bar and Kieran tried not to wince. "She lets it go to her head sometimes."

The bartender shook his head. "Nope, that's not it. I've seen Maddie West in concert and she looks nothing like you. Maddie West has long blond hair.

And she's a lot taller than you are. And a little bonier. Someone needs to feed that girl a burger or two."

"Bony? You think Maddie West is bony?" Maddie asked.

"That's a compliment," Kieran teased, giving her a playful shove. "He's paying you a compliment."

"Thank you," Maddie muttered. "That's real nice."

"My name is Jake," the bartender said as he set a menu in front of them both. "When you're ready, I'll send a waitress over."

"I think we should bowl," Maddie said after Jake wandered away. "I feel kind of conspicuous sitting here. You know, kind of...bony."

"You think you're conspicuous now? Wait until we're out there. The last time I bowled, I was—" He shook his head. "I was just a kid. We used those big bumpers on the lane. You think they'll let me use those?"

"No! But how hard can it be? You pick up the ball and roll it down the thing and then it knocks those posts down."

Kieran laughed. "You sound like an expert. The thing is an alley and those posts are pins. And I don't know how to score."

"Yeah, well, scoring has never been a problem for you," she teased. "Besides, we don't need to keep track. We'll just see how many pins we can knock down." She jumped up from her stool and grabbed his hand. "Come on. It will be fun."

Kieran picked up their belongings then grabbed his beer. They walked over to the counter and rented two pairs of shoes. Then they found their spot on the third alley.

Maddie stared down at the shoes. "I have to wear someone else's shoes? Why?"

"You can't bowl in those sandals. These are specially made to protect the alleys."

"But they're really ugly," she said. "And who knows what kind of germs are in there." She lifted them up and sniffed them, then shook her head.

"They've been disinfected," Kieran assured her. "Unfortunately, you're not allowed to bowl without them."

"But I don't have socks. I'm not putting my bare feet inside those shoes."

"Then go buy a pair of socks," he said. "They had some at the counter."

She held out her hand and he gave her some cash. "More," she said, wiggling her fingers.

By the time she returned, Kieran had his shoes on and had selected a ball. She sat down, placing a shoe box between them. "What's that?"

"I bought my own shoes," she said. "I'm not putting someone else's smelly old things on my feet. And if you bring up the expense, I'm going to throw the old ones at your head."

They spent the next hour drinking beer, munching on fried food and trying to bowl. Kieran couldn't remember the last time he'd laughed so hard. They were both ridiculously bad, rarely keeping the ball out of the gutter. There was one high point, though. Maddie slipped as she released the ball and rolled a perfect strike. Of course, she couldn't do it again.

It amazed him they could enjoy something so simple. He'd always assumed that the whole purpose of dating was to impress a woman with how cool and sophisticated he was. He'd never approached it as a chance to have fun. Maybe he'd just been dating the wrong kind of women.

"This is for the game," Maddie said, pointing to the score projected above the lane. "It's 31 to 29. If I knock down three pins, I think I'll beat you."

She rolled her first ball down the alley and it clattered into the gutter. Dejected, she returned and plopped down next to him. "You win," she conceded.

"You get another ball," he said, pointing to the scoreboard.

"Really?"

Kieran nodded. "And when you throw, try not to twist your wrist as you let the ball go. I think that's why it always goes in the thing."

"The gutter," she said. Maddie held the ball up in front of her face. "See, this is how you do it." She took three steps and rolled the ball down the lane. To Kieran's surprise, it stayed in the center and knocked down nine pins.

Their celebration was short-lived. Jake appeared a few moments later with his offer of a ride and

Kieran and Maddie gathered up their things and hurried outside.

"So, you folks want the Enterprise out at the airport or my buddy with the used-car lot?"

"We should probably stick with Enterprise," Kieran said. "Then we can return the car anywhere we want."

Jake nodded. "I see your point."

They drove down a long avenue, lined with commercial buildings and restaurants. Kieran glanced back at Maddie who sat in the backseat of the extended cab. She stared out the window, her brow furrowed, her expression unreadable.

"We really appreciate this," Kieran said. "We sort of got off the train, not knowing what was—"

"Stop!" Maddie cried.

Jake slammed on the brakes and the pickup skidded to a stop. "What?" he shouted.

"We'll get out here," Maddie said. She grabbed her bag from beside her and pushed on the back of Kieran's seat. "Here. Right here."

Kieran looked around. "There's nothing here but a couple of used car—"

"I've decided against renting a car," Maddie said. "I want to buy one."

"Well, if you're lookin' to buy a car, then I got to take you to see my buddy. He'll give you a real good deal. His place is just a mile down the road."

"All right," Maddie said. "Let's go."

A few minutes later, they both hopped out of the

truck. "You just tell Ernie that Jake sent you. He'll give you a good deal." The bartender waved as he drove off, leaving them both standing on the sidewalk.

"What the hell are we doing?" Kieran asked.

"I don't have a car. I want to learn how to drive. So I think it's about time I buy one." She smiled at him. "Good plan, right?"

"A used car?"

"Hey, you're starting to rub off on me. A new car would cost too much. A used car costs less." She grabbed his hand and pulled him along across the street.

"Maddie, you don't just buy a car on a whim. You have to shop around, especially with used cars. A new car would be more dependable, it would have a warranty and be more fuel efficient and—"

"Stop," Maddie said. "Look at all these cars. I'm sure I can find something I like here."

A crazy mixture of cars littered the lot. Kieran didn't know where to start. "Are you sure you have enough money—"

"Stop worrying about money!" Maddie cried. "I have enough to buy a used car."

"Do you have any idea how much one of these costs?"

"Less than a new car. And I suppose it would depend upon how used the car was. I'll know what I want when I see it."

Kieran pulled her to a stop and took her guitar

from her hand, setting it at her feet. "Here's the deal. Buying a used car is a risky proposition at best. You don't know anything about cars. So, this time around, rather than buying whatever strikes your fancy, I want you to take some advice. Do you think you can do that?"

"Yes," Maddie said, nodding in agreement. "I'll let you do all the talking."

The salesman introduced himself and Kieran mentioned they were looking for a good deal on a car and that Jake had directed them here. Maddie had already wandered off to look on her own. "We're looking for something that gets good mileage, easy to drive. It has to have air and a decent sound system. Maybe an SUV. Or a sporty sedan. I'm not—"

"I want this one!" Maddie shouted. "Right over here."

He and Ernie both turned to find her pointing to an old Cadillac convertible in a startling shade of bubblegum-pink. Kieran walked over to her, Eddie hard on his heels.

"This is the one," Maddie said. "How much is it?"

"Why, that's fifteen thousand," Ernie said. "Now that's a real nice car. Vintage, low miles. It was owned by a nice young lady from over in Crown Point. Her boyfriend, an older gentleman, bought it for her and had it all tuned up and painted. They broke up and he sold it to me. It's a classic Caddy. Convertible, tail fins, smooth ride."

"I love it," Maddie said, her eyes bright, her smile infectious.

Kieran grabbed her arm. "Could you excuse us for a moment? We just need to discuss a few things."

"Right," Ernie said. "I'm just going to go get the keys so you can take it for a test drive. You're gonna love it."

Kieran watched him leave, then bent close to Maddie. "I thought you were going to let me do the talking."

"I was. But then I saw this car. It's a sign. I have to have it. It's a pink Cadillac."

"I can see that."

"You know. The song, 'Pink Cadillac'? I sang it on my first album. This is the car for me. I want this one."

"It's pink, it's forty years old, it probably gets about five miles to the gallon and it's got rear wheel drive which will be impossible on ice and snow."

"Well, I like pink, it's vintage, I'm not going to drive it cross country so I don't care how much gas costs, and I just won't drive when it snows. I want you to buy this one for me." She reached into her pocket and gave him her debit card. "There's more than enough in the account to cover it," she added.

"At least let me check it out?"

Maddie nodded, watching nervously as Kieran slowly circled the car, examining it closely. "It looks clean, no rust."

"The interior is spotless," Ernie said, returning

with the keys. "And the engine purrs like a kitten. It was overhauled at 30,000 miles."

"A kitten," Maddie said. "It's a beautiful car."

"It's a car," Kieran agreed. "But it's pink. That's going to hurt the resale value."

"It's cute," Maddie insisted, her arms crossed over her chest.

"Yeah," the salesman said. "We get that comment a lot. Not the cute thing, but the re-sale value. So, let me cut off a thousand from the sticker price. I'll give it to you for fourteen."

"We'll take it," Maddie said.

"No, we won't," Kieran countered. "Not until we take it for a spin."

She gave Kieran a seductive smile as she ran her hand over the white leather seat. "Baby, don't you wonder what it feels like in the back of my pink Cadillac? See, this car is sexy. This is my car."

Kieran groaned inwardly as he stepped closer. Was it even worth trying to rein her in? If she wanted to blow her money on a pink car, who was he to complain? "It does have a nice big backseat," he conceded in a low voice. "But you can't let him know you love it."

"Why not?" she whispered.

"Because, it's all part of the art of negotiation," he said. "Leave it to me. You never pay full price for a used car."

"But he just gave us a thousand off. If you negotiate me out of this car, you're going to have to do some talking to get yourself back into my good graces," she warned. "And that includes the bedroom. Now, are you willing to take that risk?"

"I'll keep that in mind. Now wipe that smile off your face and go look at that rusty old pickup. And don't say anything. Got it?"

"Got it," Maddie said.

5

"I THOUGHT YOU were going to be quiet," Kieran shouted over the sound of the wind.

They were driving south on I-65, the top down, the warm breeze blowing around them. In the west, the sky was aflame with pinks and purples as the sun set on a beautiful August day.

"Me? Quiet? You were asking the impossible. Besides, you have to admit, this car is seriously cool. It's perfect for me. It's got some attitude. And it's worth every dollar we paid for it."

"Now you just have to learn to drive it."

"And you're going to teach me," she said. "We make a good team, don't we?"

Kieran reached over and wove his fingers through the hair at her nape, pulling her toward him for a quick kiss. Maddie smiled, then sank back into the soft leather seats. How had life gone from worrisome to wonderful in just a few short days? She was happy, she was content. All the concerns that had plagued her last week had disappeared and she felt free for the first time since she was a kid.

"So where are we going?" Kieran asked. "Besides south."

"Bitney," Maddie said. "I want to see my grandparents. I'm growing tired of the road. And since you're going to teach me to drive, I'm going teach you how to ride a horse."

He nodded. "All right. If we don't stop, we can probably get there sometime after midnight. Do you need to call your grandparents and let them know you're coming?"

"That would require turning on my phone," she said. "And I just don't want to look at it yet."

"Then why don't we find a place to stay tonight and we'll surprise them tomorrow morning?"

Maddie nodded. "Hey, I'm sorry I messed up your negotiations for the car. I'm sometimes a little impatient. But, I promise I'll let you negotiate next time. I won't say a word."

"I suppose I should just be happy that we didn't buy six cars so you could try them all out before you decided which one you wanted."

"Ha, ha," she said. "You think you know me so well, don't you?"

"There is one thing," Kieran said, reaching out to grab her hand. He pulled it to his lips and kissed her wrist. "That card you gave me to pay for the car. It was for a Sarah M. Westerfield. And that's the name you signed."

"I'm named after my grandmother," she said. "My middle name is Madeline. My mother thought Sarah Westerfield wasn't a good name for a country star so from the time I was fourteen, she's been calling me Maddie West."

"Sarah," he said. "I like that. But I think I'm going to have to stick with Maddie."

"My grandparents still call me Sarah sometimes," she said. "I don't always answer to that name though."

"Tell me about them," he said. "Do they live near Bitney?"

Maddie nodded. "About fifteen miles. It isn't far. There's not a lot in Bitney. A feed store, a few taverns, a post office. Oh, and Charlie Morgan's place. It's a roadhouse."

"And your grandparents have a horse farm?"

"It's not a regular horse farm, where they breed horses. Although, my grandfather used to train racehorses at the farm. But now, it's more like a retirement home for horses."

Kieran glanced over at her, frowning. "A retirement home? I didn't know there were such things."

"When a horse gets too old or is injured, there are only two places for it to go. The glue factory, which is a euphemism for something I refuse to talk about. Or a farm, like my grandparents' place. They take horses that no one wants anymore. Those that are injured, they rehabilitate and then sell to people who want them for recreational riding. Some just live on the farm until they die of natural causes."

"Wow. That's pretty amazing."

"My mother doesn't know it, but I send them all my royalty money. The farm is ridiculously expensive to run, but they have plenty of money to buy feed and vet care."

"Your mom wouldn't like that?"

"She and my grandparents don't exactly get along. They wanted her to go to college and she wanted to run off and start a singing career in Nashville. As soon as she was eighteen, she left home. But it didn't go well for her and she ended waiting tables. Then, she got pregnant with me and came back to Kentucky for a while, but couldn't leave the career behind. So we went back to Nashville. She got a job for a management company after I started school and things just grew from there."

"What about your dad?"

Maddie paused. She'd been thinking about her father a lot lately. She wasn't sure why. Maybe it was because she was finally free to track him down. "I never knew my father. I don't think my mother really did either. I've always suspected that I was the result of a one-night stand, although she never really said for sure. She always wanted a career in music and when I came along, I ruined that for her. So she decided to make me into a country singer instead. Unfortunately for me, I was good at it. That's how I ended up here."

"Did you ever think of finding your dad?" Kieran asked.

"Not until recently," she said. "But my mother gets really emotional when I ask about him. I'm starting to think she didn't tell me the whole story. Maybe he's married or maybe he's just some lowlife." She sighed softly. "When I was younger, I used to dream he was a big country star and I'd inherited his talent. Someday I'll ask her to tell me everything."

"When was the last time you saw your grand-parents?"

"A couple years ago," she said. "I call them on holidays and their birthdays, but they objected to me starting a career so early. They thought I needed to focus on school and have a normal life until I was eighteen. So things have been kind of tense between them and my mom. Sometimes it's better not to rock the boat."

They continued to drive another two hours and just after ten, they pulled off the interstate and found a hotel room for the night.

After checking in, they took the elevator up to the third floor, Maddie yawning as she watched the lighted buttons on the panel. "It's been a long day," she murmured. "Can you believe we started in Topeka this morning?"

"It's been fun," he said, reaching out to pull her body against his. "But I'm not going to lie. I really just want to take off all my clothes and crawl into bed with you."

Maddie had been so afraid to face life on her own, so certain that she wouldn't know what to do. But then she'd found Kieran and he'd changed everything. They'd settled into an easy relationship, with only the occasional silly conflict.

Maddie had thought that falling in love was always fraught with emotional upheaval, yet, it was so simple with Kieran. Every moment they spent together convinced her that this was much more than just a passing infatuation.

But how would they work out the details of a relationship when there was so much distance between them? He had a job, a family, in Seattle. And her life revolved around Nashville. Even if she did give up touring and recording, was she ready to pick up and move to a brand-new city?

Kieran opened the door to the room and waited as she walked inside. She dropped the guitar case near the closet, then turned and took the bags from him, setting them on the floor at his feet.

Without speaking, Maddie slowly began to undress him, unbuttoning his shirt and pushing it over his shoulders. Kieran smiled at her sleepily, unzipping the sweatshirt to reveal the pretty cotton dress beneath.

This was all she really needed to be happy, Maddie mused. This man, his voice, his kiss, his naked body beside her in bed. Like breathing and eating, he'd become a basic need for her continued existence.

Food, water, air, Kieran. She closed her eyes as he leaned forward and kissed her.

As the kiss spun out, they worked at the rest of their clothes, shedding them piece by piece until they were both naked. He picked her up and wrapped her legs around his waist, then carried her to the bed. Holding her, he gently set her down on the mattress and stretched out above her.

He really was a handsome man, she mused, staring into his pale blue eyes. He was smart and funny and sweet and kind. And he really didn't care that she was famous or rich. He liked her for who she was.

Maddie had never been able to trust another person completely. Not even the people who were supposed to be looking after her best interests—her agent, her manager, her producer. They all answered to her mother, who had been the ultimate authority.

But she could trust Kieran. How strange was that? She only just met him a few days ago, yet she sensed that he was someone who would always be on her side.

"I like this," Maddie said, brushing his dark hair from his eyes. "It's the perfect way to end the day."

"We're not doing anything," Kieran said.

"I don't need to do anything," Maddie said. "I just need you near me."

"How close?" he asked. He was already hard, his erection pressed against her belly. He moved above her, teasing at her entrance until she could think of nothing but the moment when he'd bury himself inside her.

"Closer," she murmured. She whispered softly in his ear, telling him what she wanted him to do, enticing him with words.

When he groaned softly, she knew that he couldn't wait much longer. He nuzzled her neck, kissing and biting softly, moving above her in a slow, erotic dance. Maddie reached between them to caress his shaft, now hard and ready.

"I have to get a condom," he whispered.

"I don't want you to leave me," she said.

"I'm just going across the room." He chuckled softly. "I promise, I'll come right back."

The moment he broke contact, she felt the loss—of his heat, of his desire, of the comfort that his nearness brought her. But a moment later, he returned. Maddie took the box from his hands and after tearing open the plastic package, smoothed the latex over his shaft.

He entered her slowly, the sensation so exquisite that it took her breath away. Everything seemed to be operating at half-speed between them. Time had ceased to exist and the outside world had gone dark and quiet. This was all that mattered, Maddie thought to herself as he began to move.

Nothing in her life would ever be the same. From now on, she would live knowing that there was a man who was her perfect match in passion and pleasure. Every moment between them was a revelation, a discovery of the power of sexual attraction and simple affection.

It was more than enough…for now.

THE CADILLAC BEGAN to overheat about an hour after they got back on the road the next morning. Kieran pulled off the freeway and parked the car on the edge of the country road, letting it cool down before he started it again.

Maddie perched on the back of the front seat as he peered beneath the hood. "What's wrong with it?"

"I don't know," Kieran said, wiping his hands on his jeans. "Maybe something wrong with the thermostat or the radiator. The belts look okay. It might be the water pump, although I'm not even sure this thing has a water pump."

"Could it be all of those things?" Maddie cried. "Maybe we should just replace the whole engine."

Kieran chuckled. "Maybe it's just one of those things. But we're going to have to get it looked at. It's nothing I can fix." He slammed the hood, then returned to the driver's-side door. "We'll try starting it after it cools down. If it overheats again, we'll have to call a tow truck."

He was tempted to tell Maddie that something like this was to be expected when you don't do your homework at a used-car lot. But she'd been so pleased with her purchase. And he'd been happy for her.

In truth, that's all he really cared about. Making Maddie deliriously happy. Maybe that wasn't exactly what his grandfather was hoping for when he sent his grandsons out to find a new life. But for Kieran, it wasn't about the place or the job. It was about finding someone who meant something, someone to build a life around.

Kieran imagined his brothers. New Mexico, Wisconsin, Maine. What were they doing now? Where were they living, who had they met? He couldn't imagine any of them tangled up in a relationship already.

They were probably doing as expected, examining their choices, making decisions about their futures, learning more about themselves. And here he was, driving around in a bubblegum-pink Cadillac with a runaway country singer. He could imagine the laughter that would accompany that admission.

Still, it would have been nice to have his brothers around. They might be able to help him untangle his feelings for Maddie. The longer they were together, the more he realized that things would not remain so simple. And advice was in short supply.

It was easy to ignore the future when he and Maddie were on some kind of endless road trip. They weren't really concerned about getting to their destination. In truth, they'd been avoiding it. But every trip came to an end sometime....

"Why don't you sing me a song while we're waiting?" he said.

"No, I'm not ready to sing for you," Maddie said, shaking her head.

"Why not? I'm a good audience. And I've heard you're a pretty good singer."

She shook her head. "Nope. But I will teach you how to play the guitar." Maddie crawled over the back of the seat and grabbed her guitar from the case. "Come back here. There's more room."

Kieran jumped over the seat and settled next to her. She patiently went through the parts of the guitar, the neck, the frets, the strings, the sound hole.

"Each of the strings is a different note. When you press the string down against the fret, it shortens the string and makes the pitch higher. So, when I put this combination of fingers down, it's a D chord." She handed him the guitar and put his fingers in the correct spots. "Now strum everything but the top string."

He did as she asked and a pleasant sound vibrated off the strings. Kieran ran his thumb across them again. "Don't move your fingers too close to the frets. Now shift your index and middle finger up a string and strum them all. That's an A-seventh chord."

Before long he was able to move back and forth between the two chords quite easily. "Now what?"

"Now we're going to sing a song," Maddie said. "Something simple. 'Jimmy Crack Corn.' Do you know that one?"

Kieran shook his head. "Nope."

"'Row, Row, Row Your Boat'?"

"That one I know."

He strummed the D chord and Maddie showed him where to change. Though he'd never been much of a singer, she seemed to bring out the best in him. After they mastered the first song, she sang "Jimmy Crack Corn" with him and then followed it with "Pink Cadillac."

"See, you're good already."

He pulled her into a kiss. "You're the one that's good. You're amazing. I know people tell you that all the time, but it's true."

Maddie met his gaze, searching his eyes for the truth in his words. A smile spread across her face. "For the first time, I think I believe it."

"Put your guitar away. I think the engine's cooled down enough that we can make it into town."

He slipped back behind the wheel and when she jumped onto the seat behind him, he started the car. They found a discount store with an automotive department on the edge of town and Kieran left the car parked outside one of the garage doors.

He locked their things in the trunk before they walked inside. As he was filling out paperwork, Maddie wandered off, looking for a couple of cold drinks for them both. He watched as she walked away, smiling to himself.

In a lot of ways, he hoped it would take a day or two to fix the car. He didn't want their road trip to end. He wasn't sure what awaited them at her grandparents place, but he liked having her all to himself.

"Pretty lady," the guy behind the counter said.

"Yeah, she is."

"You know who she looks like?"

Kieran nodded. "Yeah. Everyone says that."

"My wife loves that Maddie West."

"So do I," Kieran said. "So do I."

Kieran took a seat in the waiting area and grabbed a magazine sitting on the table next to him. It was a brand-new issue of a tabloid and he scanned the front page looking for Bigfoot stories. But instead, his gaze fell on a headline with a familiar name.

"'Desperately Seeking Maddie West,'" he read.

"I bought us snacks, too."

He glanced up to see Maddie approaching with a bag. She plopped down beside him and pulled out a package of red licorice. "I've been craving red licorice." She pulled out a bottle of soda. "I got you root beer. And a Coke. And a fruit punch."

He held out the tabloid to her. "I think your mother has gone to the press," he said, pointing to the headline.

Maddie stared down at the paper, then grabbed it from him, flipping through the pages until she found the story. "'Country star Maddie West took off for parts unknown after the final concert of her tour in Denver. She's been missing for four days and though her manager and mother, Constance West, has been worried, she doesn't believe that Maddie has come to any harm. West says her daughter has been suffering under the stress of touring and recording almost nonstop since the age of fourteen. But sources say the problems may run deeper and could include drugs or alcohol. Maddie West is due to begin work on her newest album in a week.'" She drew a ragged breath. "Great. Now everyone thinks I need to go to rehab. You know, my mother once said that a star isn't a star unless they've gone through terrible times in their lives. She actually said people become more popular if they've been knocked down a few times. The 'Comeback Effect' she called it. I can see her mind working right now. If I want to take time off she's going to spin it as some kind of breakdown. And then, I'm going to make a comeback, triumphing over my troubles. Oh, it's going to sell millions of records."

Maddie threw the tabloid on the floor. He grabbed her hand and gave it a squeeze. "This doesn't change anything," Kieran said. "You're exactly the same person you were ten minutes ago."

"I—I need to take a walk. How long is it going to be for the car?"

"They haven't told me yet."

"I'll be back," she said. "I just need to clear my head."

"I'll go with you," Kieran said.

"No. I'll be fine. This is kind of new for me, having time to myself. Time to think without someone following me around asking if I'm feeling all right." She bent down and kissed him, then pointed to the bag sitting beside him. "Have some treats. And throw that magazine away before anyone sees it."

She walked out the door and Kieran stood. He rang the bell on the counter and the manager appeared a few seconds later. "I'm just going to take a little walk. I'll be back soon."

"No problem," the man said.

Kieran followed Maddie out the door, keeping a safe distance. If she needed him, he'd be there for her. And if not, then at least he wouldn't be stuck sitting in the automotive department wondering where she was and if she was safe.

"I must be in love," Kieran muttered. "Either that or I'm going a little crazy."

WITH A NEW thermostat and a new lease on life, the Cadillac pulled into the long driveway of Serenity Farm around suppertime. Maddie felt her excitement grow as Kieran pulled the car to a stop.

He glanced over at her. "Are you all right?"

Maddie nodded. "My mother and I have never really settled down. We moved all the time. This is the closest thing I've ever had to a home."

The sprawling white clapboard house was exactly as she remembered it with its wide porch and deep green shutters. Her grandmother's flower gardens were lush with late-summer blooms and Maddie closed her eyes and inhaled the scent, oddly familiar.

She hadn't seen her grandparents for almost two years. And though she spoke to them on the phone once a month, it wasn't the same. She stepped out of the car at the same time that the front screen door opened.

"Hi, Ninny," she cried as she ran up the steps and embraced her grandmother. "Pawpaw, you look as handsome as ever," Maddie said as her grandfather emerged from the house. She gave him a fierce hug, then stepped back.

"You're home," her grandmother said.

"I'm home," Maddie repeated. She turned and motioned to Kieran. "This is Kieran Quinn. My friend. My…boyfriend."

Kieran took the front steps two at a time and held out his hand to her grandmother. "It's a pleasure to meet you." He shook her grandfather's hand. "Mr. Westerfield. Mrs. Westerfield."

"I'm Sarah," her grandmother said. "And this is Joe."

Kieran nodded. "Sarah. Joe. You have a beautiful place here."

"Joe, get the bags. Come in, you two. We're just finishing dinner. Are you hungry?"

Kieran helped Maddie's grandfather with the bags, dropping them both along with her guitar in the front hall. Maddie wandered back to the kitchen, the smell of dinner filling her senses.

"What's for dinner?" Maddie asked.

"Fried chicken, potato salad, green beans from my garden and sweet tea. Peach cobbler for dessert. I found the best peaches at the fruit stand yesterday. Straight from Georgia." She slipped her arm through

Maddie's and led her to the table. "What are you doing here? I thought you were on tour."

Maddie sat down and Kieran joined her a few minutes later as her grandmother fetched them both a plate. "The tour is finished. We did the last show in Denver a few days ago."

"So you have some time off?" her grandfather asked. "You'll be staying for a few days, I hope."

Maddie paused. "More than that. Maybe. I need a break. Maybe a permanent break. I just don't love it anymore."

Her grandmother poured them both a glass of tea, then placed her hand on Maddie's shoulder. "I can't say I'm surprised. Although I never thought you'd last as long as you did. You've been working nonstop for ten years. No one can put up with that kind of pressure for so long."

Maddie glanced over at Kieran and he smiled at her. "I feel much better now."

They chatted over dinner about the tour, about her trip home, but they avoided the subject of her mother. Maddie knew that Ninny wanted to bring it up, but she'd never talk about it in front of a stranger. And to her grandparents, Kieran was a stranger.

After they finished dinner, Sarah cleared the table. "Let's have our dessert on the porch a bit later. Joe, why don't you give Kieran a tour of the farm. I want to have a little talk with Maddie."

Kieran gave her hand a squeeze, then got up from the table and followed her grandfather to the front door. Maddie drew a deep breath and then sighed softly. Right now, she could use a few moments alone with Kieran, but those were going to be hard to find until her grandparents were in bed.

"He seems like a nice boy," Sarah said. "Where did you meet him?"

"In the bus station in Denver," Maddie said. "He helped me escape. And we've been together ever since."

"So you've known him…"

"Four days," she said. "I know, it seems like nothing. But we have such a strong connection."

"And what does he do, besides drive runaway country singer home to visit her grandparents?"

"He works for his family business in Seattle. They build boats. Expensive sailing yachts."

"And he's on vacation?"

Maddie shrugged. "Something like that. He's taking time away, like I am."

"Well, I'm not going to ask the particulars, but I think it's best if he sleeps in the stable house."

"I think I might be falling in love with him," Maddie said. "He's so kind and sweet and funny. And he cares about me. Not me, the country singer, but me, just plain old Sarah Madeline Westerfield."

"Your mother isn't going to be happy about that," Sarah said. "But I can see how he looks at you. I'm going to reserve judgment until I get to know him a little better."

"You're going to like him. I know it."

"Does your mother know you're here?"

Maddie shook her head. "I'm sure she'll figure it out at some point. Kieran texted her to let her know I was all right but I know she's going to be crazy until she talks to me. I was going to call her, but then I chickened out. You know how she likes to control every little thing."

"Your mother has made mistakes," Sarah said. "I'll be the first one to point that out. But you do have a wonderful career, sweetheart. And you're so talented. I wasn't behind this when you were just a teenager, but now, I listen to you sing and I know you're doing exactly what you should be doing."

"Am I?" Maddie said. She pushed away from the table. She'd expected her grandmother to side with her, not her mother. But now it sounded as if they both thought she should go back. "I'm not sure I want to go back. I think maybe I want something else out of life. Is that so wrong, to want an ordinary life?"

"Does that ordinary life include being married to Kieran Quinn? Sometimes love can make us think in fairy tales instead of realities. If you're counting on this young man to rescue you from all your troubles, then I think you need to reconsider your options."

Was that what she was doing? Maddie wondered. Her grandmother had always urged her to take control of her own life and until now, she hadn't found the courage to do that. But the courage hadn't been all her own. Kieran had helped.

"I don't expect that," Maddie said. "He has a job

and a life in Seattle. He'll have to go home and I'll have to make some decisions about what I want."

"Well, sweetheart, I think you need to take your time. You're a big girl now."

Maddie stood up. "You know, I think I'm going to catch up with Kieran. Why don't you leave the dishes and Kieran and I will do them later?"

She was anxious to get out of the kitchen, away from all of her grandmother's questions, away from the mirror that Sarah Westerfield held up to Maddie's face. She wanted to grab her things and throw them back in the car, to run away again. When she was with Kieran, she didn't have to think about her future. She could just live each day without concern for the next.

She found Kieran and her grandfather standing at the gate to the stable paddock, watching a pair of horses gallop around the perimeter, their tails and manes flying. She stood next to Kieran, wrapping her arms around him.

"Have you met all the horses?" she asked.

"Some of them," Kieran said. "I've never really been around horses. They're much bigger than I thought they'd be. Close up, I mean."

"We'll have our first riding lesson tomorrow," Maddie said. "You wait. You'll be a pro before you know it."

"I guess that means I'm going to have to take you driving."

Her grandfather chuckled. "Our Maddie behind

the wheel. Oh, dear. We tried that once and it didn't come out well."

"I went off the driveway and into the pasture fence," Maddie said. "I mixed up the brake with the gas." She smiled, remembering. "But I was only thirteen."

"Hopefully, the last eleven years have taught you the difference between go and stop," her grandfather said. "But your inability to tell left from right never stopped me from loving you, darlin'." He turned away from the fence and gave her a kiss. "Take a look around. You helped build this farm, Maddie West. Look what your music has made for us." He cleared his throat and Maddie caught sight of a tear in his eye. "Well, I'm hungry for a piece of your grandmother's cobbler. And then, I'm going to listen to the ball game."

"Pawpaw is a big baseball fan," Maddie explained. "Braves all the way."

"I'm a Mariners fan myself," Kieran said.

"I do like my ball games," Joe said. He gave them both a wave as he walked away, his hands shoved in his pockets.

Kieran draped his arm around Maddie's shoulders and then pulled her into a long and lazy kiss. "I've missed that," he murmured against her lips. "I feel like I have to be on my best behavior."

"You better be. Ninny is putting you out in the stable house. I think she knows we've been sleeping together. She won't have any of that premarital sex under her roof."

"So we'll have to find another roof?"

"The backseat of the car is made for fun," Maddie said.

He kissed her again. "Can you sneak out after everyone is asleep?"

Maddie groaned softly. "Now I'm wishing we'd stayed on the train."

"We'll be fine," Kieran said.

"I hope so," Maddie said, burying her face in his chest. Though she'd been happy to see her grandparents again, Maddie couldn't help but sense that the fantasy that she and Kieran had been living had come to an end.

Sooner or later, she'd have to make some decisions about her future. When she was with Kieran, that always seemed so far off. But now, here with her family, her responsibilities seemed to come rushing back, full force.

6

KIERAN SAT ON the front steps of the stable house, a long, low building that housed four identical rooms. Each had a small galley kitchen, a sitting area with a fireplace and a comfortable bed, one that seemed very empty without Maddie.

He stared up at the main house, wondering which room was hers. The lights had been turned off long ago, the only illumination coming from the porch. He closed his eyes and laid back on the cool wood of the porch floor.

Though it was nice to see Maddie with her grandparents, he much preferred their time on the road. He'd had her completely to himself and it was a luxury that he missed already. She'd barely left his side for four straight days and now they were separated by a hundred yards at the most. It might as well have been a hundred miles.

He glanced at his watch. It was already past midnight. She'd probably been so exhausted she'd fallen asleep. Maybe it was time for him to give up and turn in himself. Kieran pushed to his feet and pulled the screen door open.

A ceiling fan whirred above his head, keeping the room cooler than the outside temperature, which had to be close to eighty. He wore only his boxers, but it wasn't enough. His skin was covered by a light sheen of perspiration.

He flopped down on the bed and stared up at the ceiling, watching the fan blades as they created a blur of movement. Though it had taken him a bit longer to reach his destination, Kieran knew he'd have to start making some plans of his own.

He couldn't continue sponging off of Maddie and he wasn't about to take advantage of her grandparents either. Tomorrow morning, he'd have to find work. He'd drive into Bitney and see what his original destination had to offer.

Kieran drew a deep breath and let it out slowly. Hell, he'd rather jump back in the car and head off on another road trip with Maddie. They'd had so much fun together, living without a care in the world.

But now, he felt a distance between them. They were back in the real world, where running away became an irresponsible act and sleeping with a lover was beyond the bounds of propriety.

He closed his eyes, hoping that sleep would come quickly. But the heat was making it almost impossible to relax. Still, he must have dozed off because the next thing he knew, Maddie was crawling into bed beside him.

Her hand skimmed down his chest before her fingers wrapped around his shaft. At first, Kieran though he might be dreaming. But the sensations were too intense, too real to be happening only in his mind.

Kieran rolled onto his side and looked at her in the dim light from the beside lamp. "Hi," he murmured.

"Hi," she replied.

He kissed her softly. In a single moment, the world was right again. They were together, lying next to each other, able to touch and talk at will.

She wore a thin cotton nightgown, barely a barrier to his touch. Kieran ran his hand along her arm, her skin like silk beneath his touch. Over the past few days, he'd come to know her body so well, but his response to her presence always surprised him. Every moment together was a chance to discover something new and amazing.

His hand drifted lower, to her hip and then her thigh. The breeze from the fan fluttered at her nightgown and Kieran caught the fabric in his fingers and slowly drew it up along her leg, revealing the perfect curve of her backside. Each new spot of naked skin was a revelation, a place to explore and appreciate.

The heat had slowed everything, including his seduction, to an indolent pace. But Maddie didn't seem to mind. When he found the spot between her legs, she sighed softly and parted her thighs, arching into his touch as if it were an instinctual reaction.

She was already damp with desire and he fought the urge to pull her beneath him and drive deep and hard. The need to completely possess her had become necessary for his survival and the experience of losing himself inside her fed that obsession.

Maddie grazed the front of his boxers with her fingertips. He was already hard, his erection straining against the cotton. As she slipped her hand beneath the waistband and wrapped her fingers around him again, Kieran held his breath, fighting the surge of desire that nearly overwhelmed him.

Would it ever be possible to walk away from this? In his wildest imagination, he couldn't fathom a single reason for letting her go. They belonged together. This passion and the pleasure that soon would follow, was what life was supposed to be about.

"Make love to me," Maddie whispered as she stroked him.

He reached for the box of condoms that he'd left on the bedside table, but she stopped him, grabbing the box from his hand and tossing it across the room. "I just want you," she said.

Kieran wasn't sure how to respond. The thought of moving inside her without a barrier between them sent another flood of heat through his bloodstream. "Are you all right? I mean, are you—"

"I have that covered."

With a soft groan, he pulled her beneath him,

dragging her nightgown up around her waist. He found her lips again, desperate to taste her. No matter how close they were, it never seemed to be enough.

Over the past few days, they'd been physically inseparable, but there had still been an emotional distance that they both kept. But now, he felt that distance slowly dissolving. Was this what it was like to fall in love?

She was like no other woman he'd ever known. In the past, women had been a pleasurable diversion, a necessary component to deep sexual satisfaction. A warm body, a sweet mouth.

But Maddie was so much more. She was a companion, a friend. A lovely presence in his life that he didn't want to lose. Kieran pressed his lips to her neck, then moved down her body, first to her breast and then to the soft flesh of her belly.

There was nothing about her that he didn't find addictively beautiful. How had he lived so long without ever knowing her? If he'd seen her CDs in a store or happened upon a photo of her in a magazine, would he have felt an instant connection? Were they always meant to be together like this? Or would they have spent the rest of their lives searching for each other?

Maddie ran her fingers through his hair and gently guided him back to her mouth. When he'd settled himself between her legs, she caught the waistband of his boxers in her thumbs and tugged them down around his hips. Kieran knew that he was already dancing close to the edge. Every nerve in his body was alive with anticipation. The tip of his shaft teased at her damp entrance and he held his breath, trying to maintain his control. He rocked his hips, his erection sliding against the moist slit between her legs, the contact sending his senses into overdrive.

He could feel her arching beneath him, her breath coming in quick gasps and he picked up his pace, the rhythm driving her closer to her release. She grew tense against him and Kieran knew she was close.

And when she finally cried out, he sank into her, burying himself in her enveloping warmth. Her spasms surrounded him and a moment later, after just a few strokes, he couldn't hold back any longer.

The exquisite sensation of surrender was something that he'd come to crave, but it was only with Maddie that it all made sense. This was what sex was supposed to be, an intimate joining of souls and hearts, not just physical satisfaction. All those other women, those other times, meant nothing to him.

They lay beside each other for a long time, waiting for their bodies to recover. Kieran toyed with a strand of her hair, twisting it around his finger. He opened his mouth to speak, then drew a sharp breath, wondering how to broach the subject.

"Don't worry," she said, as if she could read his mind. "We didn't need a condom."

"Since when?"

Maddie drew back and looked into his gaze, smiling. "Since before I met you. This isn't my first rodeo, you know." She shrugged. "My mother was a teenage mom. The first time I looked at a boy, she dragged me to the doctor. I knew all about the birds and the bees early on and let me tell you, my friends at school wanted to hear all about it. Though I didn't use that vast knowledge myself until I was almost twenty."

"And how did that go?"

"It was surprisingly quick and uninspired. He played in my backup band on my summer tour. He was a drummer and I thought he was the cutest thing I'd ever seen. It lasted a week and a half. When my mother found out, she fired him. He's a studio musician now in Nashville. We run into each other every now and then. He's still pretty cute."

"Cuter than me?"

"No. But he was a gentleman. Even though he got fired, he never said anything to the press, never sold his story. I was lucky he was my first."

"Have other guys sold their stories?"

"Not completely. But they have kissed and told. Promise me you won't do that?"

Kieran gasped, stunned that she'd even think him capable of doing that. "No. Maddie, I'd never— How could you even think I'd consider—" He paused. "I promise. What's happened between us, stays between us."

She nodded. "All right, then."

He pulled her into his arms and kissed the top of her head. "Sometimes you say the silliest things."

Surely, she had to know that she could trust him, completely and without reservation. If he needed to prove anything to her, it was that. Because without trust, there was no chance that this would last.

"FIRST OF ALL this is nothing like learning to ride a horse," Kieran said. "After this morning's lesson, I can personally attest to that."

"I'm still nervous." Maddie stared at her hands gripping the steering wheel of the Cadillac.

"How do you think I felt on top of that horse?" Kieran asked. "At least with a car, you're in control. That horse had a mind of it's own."

"You just weren't decisive enough with your commands," Maddie said. "Your horse sensed that you were unsure, so he took advantage. They're very clever animals."

"Well, your car won't be doing that because it doesn't have a brain of its own. It does, however, have this nice comfortable leather seat so your butt won't hurt after a nice long ride."

She turned to him. "Your butt hurts?"

"Yeah. I'm a little sore."

"But you did well," Maddie said. "You got the hang of it right away. You just have to be more confident. We'll go riding again tomorrow morning."

"I'm not sure my backside can handle that."

"Oh, don't be such a big baby. I'll massage it for you later tonight. And you'll see, the more you do it, the better you'll get. Kind of like sex." She playfully bumped his shoulder. "I'm a good teacher, aren't I?"

"You are," Kieran said. He slipped his arm around her shoulders and pulled her close. "It really was fun, even if it was nothing like I'd imagined it would be."

"Why not?"

"I used to dream about riding when I was a kid. I used to watch horses in the movies and it looked so easy and natural. I didn't expect to feel so... vulnerable."

"So it didn't live up to your childhood dreams?"

He shook his head. "No. But then, I'm not sure anything ever does. You dreamed about being a famous country singer and that didn't live up to your dreams either, did it?" He paused. "Maybe, as we get older, our dreams change."

"What is your dream now?"

He chuckled softly. "To get you driving," he teased. "I want to see you behind the wheel of this putrid pink Cadillac, your hair blowing in the breeze, the radio playing and the scenery flying by. That's a picture I'd like to have in my mind."

Maddie fought back a lump of emotion in her throat. So his dream was to see her happy? Was that really the first thing that came to mind? She hadn't missed the fact that he wanted an image, a memory, to hold on to. And the only reason for that was if he was planning to leave.

"I know you've been worried about getting a job," she murmured. "I spoke to my grandfather and he said he'd be happy to offer you a spot here on the farm. Two of the boys that usually help out are on the high school football team and they can only put in hours on the weekends. He said he'd pay you a wage or give you room and board, it's up to you."

"That would be nice, but I—"

"We're only a few miles from Bitney," she said. "It's silly for you to go looking for work there when you can work here. And if you're here, we can still see each other a lot."

Kieran thought about her suggestion for a long moment, then nodded. "I'll talk to your grandfather tonight."

"Good. Now are we ready to drive?"

"Put your right foot on the brake. Then pull the shift lever forward and then down until the pointer is on the *D*."

"Check," she said, doing exactly as she was told.

"Now just slide your foot off the brake and gently rest it on the gas pedal. Don't push down."

The car began to slowly creep forward. Maddie tightened her grip on the steering wheel. "Now what?"

"We're just going to let it go for a bit," he said. "Just get used to moving and steering."

Maddie could have crawled faster than the car was moving. But she felt completely in control and that was good. And Kieran seemed relaxed beside her, his arm stretched out on the backseat.

They went once around the circular drive in front

of the house before Kieran spoke again. "Now, slowly press down on the brake with your right foot and we come to a stop."

They circled the drive again and again, each time going a little faster until the car glided around at a smooth speed. Maddie felt comfortable moving between the brake and the gas pedal. "Now what?" she called.

"We're ready to go," he said. "Next time, just head down the driveway."

A few seconds later, Maddie was steering down the drive, the breeze blowing her hair around her face, a feeling of exhilaration filling her with excitement. When they reached the end of the drive, Maddie glanced over at Kieran.

"Now where?"

He shrugged. "You're driving. It's your decision."

They headed out on the curving country road, cruising along at a top speed of thirty miles per hour. When a pickup truck roared up behind her, Maddie maintained her cool and waited for him to pass, not willing to let the other driver's impatience rattle her.

She took several turns, then headed down a narrow road leading toward Bluestone Lake. "I used to fish down here with my grandfather," she said. "We ride back here, too. There's a trail that leads from my grandparents place down to the lake. The man that owns the property boards his horses at the farm. Sasha and Maggie."

The road dead-ended and Maddie slowed the car

as she reached the end. When she stopped the car, she let out a tightly held breath. "All right. I think I've had enough for the first day."

"That was pretty good," he said. "Much better than my attempts at riding."

She opened her door and stepped out. The air was thick with the sounds of cicadas and birds took flight as they walked to the water. He joined her, staring out at the glassy surface of the lake. "What a great spot," he said.

They wandered down to the water's edge. Maddie bent down and grabbed a flat stone and skipped it across the water. It bounced twice before disappearing beneath the surface.

"My mother called this morning," she said.

"When?"

"When we were riding. My grandmother, who is not an accomplished liar, told her that she hadn't talked to me. So, I'm expecting that she'll turn up here in the next few days."

She picked up another stone and this time managed three skips before it sank. She risked a glance over at Kieran, only to find him watching her.

"What do you want to do? Maddie, if you want to leave, we'll go. I'll do whatever you want," he offered.

"I can't keep running," she said. "Sooner or later, I'm going to have to face her and explain my side of this."

"Do you know what you want?"

She lifted her shoulders in a vague shrug. "I feel stronger, like I can finally stand up to her. But I'm afraid that I'm not going to have a choice. How do I just walk away from a career?"

"I know how you're feeling. After six weeks, I'm supposed to go back to Seattle and make a decision that will affect the rest of my life. I'm the logical choice to run the family business. But I'm not sure that's what I want."

"You aren't?"

Kieran shook his head. He picked up another stone and handed it to her. "Nope."

They had stumbled upon the perfect affair—all fun, no strings, both of them on vacation from reality. What more could she ask for? But with each day that passed, Maddie realized that she wanted to think about a future, a happy life with a husband and a family.

And it all started when she'd met Kieran. Everything had changed that day in the bus station. She found the one person in the world who completely understood her. He found all her most annoying qualities amusing and all her most amusing qualities adorable. How could she not fall hopelessly in love with a man like that?

"Do you miss being home?" she asked.

"Yeah, a little bit," he said. "I miss hanging out with my brothers."

"I always wished I had siblings," she said. "It

must be nice. You'll always have them. Someday, I'm going to be all alone."

"No, you won't," Kieran said. "You'll be married. You'll have a family. Children and grandchildren."

A smiled twitched at her lips as she tried to imagine herself raising kids. She still felt like a kid herself. "It's hard to have a family and a singing career," she said.

"So you're thinking about going back?"

"I don't know." And truthfully, she didn't. She'd be a fool to throw away a career she'd spent ten years building. She helped to support her grandparents' farm and she employed her mother as well as a lot of other people. Like her grandmother said, she had a responsibility to use her talents. "I feel better, almost like I want to perform again. Not in a big arena show, but in a smaller venue. I think I could do that."

"I'd like to hear you sing," Kieran said. "'Jimmy Crack Corn' and 'Row, Row, Row Your Boat' weren't really that impressive."

"All right," she said. "Soon."

He drew her into his embrace and kissed her forehead. "Soon," he murmured.

A SLOW COUNTRY song from the car radio drifted on the night air, mixing with the soft sounds of the breeze in the trees. Kieran closed his eyes and leaned back into the soft leather seat of the Cadillac.

He and Maddie had driven the car out along the

narrow road between the paddocks until they found a private spot to enjoy the sunset.

"And how was your first day of work, honey?" Maddie asked.

He turned to look at her. They were both stretched out in the backseat, their bare feet propped up on the edge of the front seat. "Remember how I said I was sore from riding yesterday? That wasn't sore. This is sore."

"You're just not used to it," Maddie said, smiling.

"No kidding. I sit behind a desk all day long, in front of a computer. I read reports and talk to the accountants." Kieran groaned inwardly. He'd never actually described his job but now that he had, it sounded really boring. "You know, I never actually get anything done at work. I mean, I finish reports and take meetings, but then, the next month, it starts all over again. At least, here at the farm, I finished something."

"Maybe," Maddie said. "But you're going to do the same things tomorrow, too. Stables need to be cleaned, horses need to be fed and groomed."

"But it feels good. I work hard. I sweat. And when the day is over, I feel like I accomplished something."

"You're getting a nice tan," she said, running her hand over his bare chest.

"Don't even start," he murmured. "I'm not sure I can move."

Maddie put on a pretty pout. "You didn't use your lips today. Or your tongue. They should still work okay." She carefully climbed over him until her legs straddled his hips. Bending close, she drew her tongue along his bottom lip.

A groan slipped from his throat. Her kiss had the intended reaction. He felt himself getting hard beneath his jeans.

"You know, we're going to have to get you some country-boy clothes if you're going to be staying here. You can't keep dressing like an accountant from Seattle."

"There is a certain smell that follows me out of the barn," he said. "But I'm going to have to make a little money before I can afford clothes."

"I could take you shopping," Maddie said. "And then, after we get you looking good, I'll take you out. We'll go dancing."

"At a club?"

She laughed. "No, not at a club. I'll take you to Charlie's. It's a honky-tonk not far from here. I used to sing there when I was younger. Charlie kind of gave me my start."

"Yeah? That might be fun. But it's going to have to wait a few days, until I can actually move my arms and legs. And I'm not much of a dancer."

"You learned to ride. You can learn to dance. It's really easy. Just, quick, quick, slow, slow." She crawled off of him and jumped out of the car, then held out her hand. "Come on. Let's dance in the moonlight. I'll show you how."

Kieran glanced up at the moon in the sky above

them. It was an impossibly romantic notion. But then, over the past few days, he'd become a romantic kind of guy. He could imagine his brothers laughing at the "new" Kieran, so head-over-heels in love that he was willing to do anything to please his woman.

Wincing, he managed to get himself out of the car. When they stood facing each other, barefoot on the soft grass of the lane, Kieran slipped his arm around her waist and took Maddie's other hand in his.

"All right, this part is pretty easy," he murmured, bending close to brush his lips across her cheek. "What's next?"

"We'll start with a simple two-step," she said. "You take two quick steps and then two slow." Maddie demonstrated, her body brushing against his as they moved.

At first, they fell into the rhythm of the music quite easily. Kieran counted the rhythm in his head. But then he lost count and nearly stepped on Maddie's toe. As he stumbled to avoid it, he ended up pulling her along with him as they tumbled into the ground.

"Ow, ow, ow," he cried, the sore muscles in his body screaming in pain. "I can't do this."

Maddie rolled to his side and wrapped her arm around his waist. "All right, we'll practice later. But I *am* going to take you out dancing. Tomorrow night. Be ready. We're going to have fun."

He kissed the top of her head. "I always have fun with you, no matter what we're doing." He wanted to tell her how much she meant to him, how she'd changed his life. But it sounded so corny. They'd known each other for less than a week. It was too early to start professing his love.

Was that what he felt for her? Or was he merely infatuated? She was so stubborn and unpredictable and fearless and funny, all the things that he never thought he'd want in a woman. But every moment they spent together was new and exciting.

Neither one of them were ready to talk about the future. She had a career waiting for her and he had a life back in Seattle. He'd tried to think of a way it might work. If she gave up touring, she could come to Seattle and write songs. Or if he left Seattle, he could go out on the road with her, maybe help her manage her finances. But both of those options seemed to be a compromise for at least one of them.

Kieran reached over and cupped her cheek in his hand. "I don't want this to end," he said softly. "I feel like we've found something and I'm afraid to lose it."

She smiled. "We have had fun," she said.

Kieran nodded. "It's been more than that, Maddie. My grandfather sent me out to see new possibilities, and I have. And now, I'm not sure I want to go back to my old life."

"What would you do?" Maddie asked, her gaze fixed on his.

"I don't know yet. Drive across the country in a pink Cadillac. Swim naked in the ocean. Learn to fly a plane. There are a million things I haven't done. I thought my life was fine before. I had everything I wanted—a good job, a nice car, a cool place to live, lots of…stuff. But I don't miss it at all. That's got to tell me something."

"I feel like I've changed since I met you," Maddie said. "Maybe I've grown up a little bit."

"Yeah?"

"Yeah. And you've probably noticed that I have been a little more careful with my money. And I'm trying to be more patient and more practical. I feel stronger, like I can stand up for myself and make decisions about my life." She sighed softly. "We'll see how long that lasts once my mother shows up."

"Don't say that," he whispered. "Don't let her beat you before you've even gotten in the fight. It's your career and your life and you can do what you want."

"But it isn't really my career," Maddie said. "She built it for me. She worked so hard and sacrificed so much. And sometimes, I feel like I'm just an ungrateful child."

Kieran pulled her into a long, deep kiss, lingering over her mouth as she melted against him. She was so soft and sweet, he never wanted to stop touching her. He buried his face in her silken hair and pressed a kiss to the soft skin beneath her ear. "If your mother wants the best for you, then she'll want you to be happy."

Maddie sat up beside him, brushing away the tears that had suddenly filled her eyes. "You're right," she said. "You're always right."

"Not always," he said. "I think I may have been wrong about dancing. I'm not sure I can get up off the ground."

Maddie stood, then reached down and pulled him up by the arm. "Come on, old man. Let's find you somewhere more comfortable to enjoy the moonlight. Why don't we give that big backseat a try?"

"Maybe you should just drive me home and put me to bed," he said.

Maddie giggled. "Come on. I've never done it in the backseat of a pink Cadillac." She began to sing the song to him, slow and sexy, in a provocative voice, as they walked back to the car. She opened the passenger-side door, then pulled the seat forward, holding his hand as she stepped into the car.

Maddie turned suddenly and wrapped her hand around his waist, pulling him down onto the soft leather seat. "I've heard that all sorts of things can happen in the backseat of a car. Whatever are you going to do with me?"

"First, we're going to do a little kissing," Kieran said, dropping a soft kiss on her lips. "And then we're going to do a little touching." He slowly opened the buttons on the front of her dress.

He smoothed his hand inside the bodice and beneath the silky fabric of her bra, cupping the soft flesh of her breast in his palm. Teasing at her nipple, he brought it to a hard peak. With a soft groan, Maddie sank back into the seat, pulling him alongside her.

"Now, how did it go?"

"Quick, quick, slow, slow," she replied.

He flicked his tongue across her nipple twice then circled the peak two more times slowly. "How's that?"

"I'll never be able to dance the two-step again without thinking about this."

"Quick, quick, slow, slow," he whispered.

Maddie arched against him. "Oh, I like that. Let's try again," she said.

Desire had brought all of his senses into fine focus and he knew that he'd remember every moment of this encounter. The smells, the sounds, the sensations were all marked indelibly in his brain.

He smoothed his hand up the length of her leg, drawing her skirt up until he found the sweet spot between her legs. She was already damp and he ran a finger between her folds. Maddie arched her body toward his touch, her breath catching in her throat.

"No wonder my mama always warned me about this," she murmured.

"What did she warn you about?"

"She told me to stay out of backseats with boys." She wrapped her arms around his neck. "But since you're a man, I figure I don't have to worry about anything now, do I?"

Kieran pulled her beneath him, trapping her hands above her head. "You'd be right about that."

7

MADDIE LOOKED AT herself in the mirror, then grabbed a lipstick from the top drawer of her dresser. She smoothed on some strawberry-scented gloss, then smacked her lips together. "Better," she said.

Grabbing her sweater, she hurried down the stairs to the kitchen. When she saw her grandmother at the kitchen sink, she twirled around, showing off the pretty flowered sundress she'd found in Lexington that morning. "What do you think?"

"Lovely," her grandmother said, placing a dish in the drainer.

"Kieran and I are going out to Charlie's." She leaned over her grandmother's shoulder and gave her a kiss. "We're going dancing."

"You two have fun. And don't you dare get up on that stage and sing a song unless you call your Ninny and Pawpaw. It's been a long time since we've heard you sing."

"I promise, I'll give you both a private concert.

We'll make a big deal out of it. We'll sit on the porch and drink lemonade and you can give me a standing ovation, just like you used to."

Her grandmother laughed. "Well, that would suit me just fine."

"I gotta go," Maddie said, hurrying to the door.

"Sweetheart, wait just a moment."

Maddie paused at the screen door and turned back. "What is it?"

"Your mama called again today," Sarah said, grabbing a towel to dry her hands.

"Did you tell her I was here?"

"No, I did not. I told her it had been a while since I'd spoken to you, which it was. And I told her that the next time I spoke to you, I'd be sure to tell you to call her. Which I am. Call your mother, Sarah Madeline Westerfield. I'm not going to lie for you again."

"Thank you, Ninny. I'll be sure to call her. Just as soon as I figure out what I want to say."

"I won't lie again," her grandmother repeated as Maddie stepped out on the porch.

"There you are. I've been waiting out here for a while."

Kieran stood at the bottom of the porch steps. He was dressed in the shirt she'd bought him earlier that morning in Lexington, a plaid cotton work shirt with mother-of-pearl buttons. "Did you find a pair of boots that fit?"

He tugged up the leg of his jeans and showed off

the cowboy boots. "You bought six pair. And eight shirts."

"I can return the ones you don't like."

"I like these," he said.

"Well, you look just like a country boy, now. Where's your hat?"

He shook his head. "I'm not wearing a hat. I tried, but I look silly. The shirt and the boots are enough. The hat is just...well, that would be overkill."

"All right." She walked down the steps and ruffled her fingers through his damp hair. "You're lucky you're such a pretty boy."

He scooped her up in his arms and spun her around. "And you're lucky I like to see you smile. If my brothers saw me in this getup, I'd never hear the end of it."

"Well, they don't have to worry. With a name like Kieran, there's not much chance of you going full country on them."

He set her on her feet and they started toward the car. "What's wrong with Kieran?"

"If you're a country boy, you need two names. Like Jim-Bob or Joe-Don or Billy-Ray. What's your middle name?"

"Prescott?"

"Kieran Prescott Quinn? Really?"

"It was my mother's maiden name. All of us have that as our middle name."

"It sounds pretty stuffy to me."

"Well, what do you want to call me?" Kieran asked as he opened the car door for her.

She hooked her finger beneath his chin and gave him a quick kiss. "I'll just call you darlin'," she said with an exaggerated drawl.

Kieran got behind the wheel and started the car. "Where are we going?"

"We're going to Bitney. I figured you better at least get a look at your original destination. That's where Charlie's Roadhouse is. He's got live music and dancing and good food and cold beer. Everything a country boy could want."

"You know, someday, I'd like to see you in Seattle. I'd put you in boat shoes and a slicker and we'd head out on the Sound on a windy day."

"I've never been on a sailboat," she said. "I've gone to a few parties on big yachts. And I've sung on a cruise ship. But I've never been sailing."

"It's pretty easy. You'd just have to sit next to me and look beautiful as the wind blows your hair back. Kind of like what you're doing right now. Sailing is a lot like riding around in your Caddie. It's just done on water."

"Does your sailboat have a big backseat?"

Kieran laughed. "No, but it has a large bed in the master cabin." He reached over and grabbed her hand, then gave it a kiss. "You do have to come to Seattle some day. Promise me you will."

"I promise," Maddie said.

Maddie smiled to herself as they took off through

the warm country night. She'd tried to imagine Kieran back in Seattle, dressed in a suit and tie, sitting behind his desk, working on his reports. But no matter how she constructed the image, it never seemed to fit the man she knew.

He was so perfectly at ease in this life, as if he had been meant for it all along. And though he'd been a bit uptight when they'd first met, he'd relaxed along the way.

She thought back to all their adventures on the road. Their trip had been a honeymoon of sorts, a time when they really got to know each other. But there was still so much to learn. She didn't even know his family, and she knew little of his life in Seattle.

Maddie glanced over at him, taking in his handsome profile, illuminated by the lights from the dash. She'd been taking him for granted, assuming that he'd be with her forever. Six weeks wasn't forever. And now, there were only five weeks left. Soon, it would dwindle down even further and then they'd be saying goodbye to each other.

How would it work? Would they make plans? Would she follow him out to Seattle? Would he visit her? She didn't even have a home!

"I need to get a place of my own," Maddie said.

Kieran turned to her. "What?"

"I need to get a place to live. Of my own. A house, maybe. Or a condo. I need your help."

"All right," he said slowly. "When do you want to start looking?"

"Soon," she said. "I think I'd like to see what's available in Nashville. That would make the most sense."

"Where did you live before you went on tour?"

"With my mother. But her house is really big and not very homey. I want a place that's cozy, like my grandparents' house. Maybe something out in the country where I can have a few horses. And a dog. I've never had pets. I'd like a dog."

"All right," Kieran said. "Maybe we can go this weekend. How far is Nashville from here?"

"It takes around four and a half hours," she said.

"All right then, we'll go to Nashville." He chuckled. "It's been a long time since we've done a road trip."

"It has," Maddie said, her mood brightening. "I'm starting to get itchy feet."

"You know, I've always dreamed about taking off and sailing around the world. But now that I've had a chance to see a little more of this country, I think it would be fun to just spend a year driving."

Maddie turned in her seat, sliding closer to him. "Yes. In one of those big recreational vehicles. My mother and I used to have one of those when I first started out. During the summer, we'd drive all over, doing county fairs and firemen's picnics. It was so much fun just hopping in that thing and—"

She drew a sharp breath. It *had* been fun. And

yet she'd given him the impression that her life had been miserable, that she'd been forced into a career she never really wanted.

"What is it?" Kieran asked.

"Nothing," Maddie replied. "I was just remembering."

"Maybe we'll do that someday. I'll get us a big R.V. and we'll take off and see the country. I'll come to your new place in Nashville and grab you and your dog, then we'll go to the Grand Canyon and to Washington, D.C. and Mount Rushmore."

"I'd like to go to Boston," Maddie said. "And I've always wanted to see those giant redwoods in California."

"It sounds like a plan," Kieran said.

A plan. Was that the same as a future? Because the more she thought about it, the more she wanted a future with Kieran. She needed to know that he'd be there, to help her through the tangle that was her life. If he was with her, then she could do anything. If he was with her, she could stand on a stage in front of thousands of people and sing her songs without any fear.

Maddie turned to watch the landscape passing by in the night. Was that true? Could he help her have a singing career again? Or had she just imagined that he was some white knight coming in to save her from all her troubles?

No, she didn't need Kieran for anything. What she needed was to learn to stand on her own two feet.

THEY COULD HEAR the music from the honky-tonk as Kieran pulled the Caddy into the parking lot. He searched for a place to park and when they finally found one, Maddie reached for her door.

"Wait right there," he said. He got out and circled around, then opened the door for her with a flourish of his arm.

"Aren't you a gentleman," she teased.

"The way I see it, this is a date. I better be on my best behavior. I'm really hoping to impress you."

"But I like it when you're bad," Maddie said, slipping her arm through his.

Kieran had never been to a roadhouse, but from what he could tell, it was a country version of a dance club, with a bar, a small menu of mostly burgers and ribs, a dance floor and a stage for a band.

"Maddie West?"

They both turned to see an enormous man dressed in a shiny gold shirt approaching.

"Charlie Morgan," Maddie said, holding out her arms. "I was hoping I'd find you here tonight."

The man picked her up around the waist, giving her a fierce hug and picking her up off the ground. Kieran winced, wondering if the show of affection was at all painful.

Charlie set her back down on her feet. "Gosh, look at you. I haven't seen you for…how long?"

"A couple years," she said. "I stopped by the last time I was at my grandparents' place."

"How are Ninny and Pawpaw?" Charlie asked.

"They're great," she said.

"And I don't have to ask how you are. We all know." He glanced around at the patrons gathered nearby. "Look who we have here, folks. Maddie West has stopped by to say hello."

The crowd erupted in shouts and applause. But this time, Maddie didn't seem to mind the attention. She smiled and waved at them. "I just had to stop by my favorite place in the world," she called out, playing the crowd. This brought more applause.

"I hope you're plannin' to sing a song or two tonight," Charlie said.

Maddie shrugged. "We'll see. I aim to do a little dancing. Maybe drink a few beers and have one of those artery-clogging burgers of yours."

"Bar or booth?" Charlie asked.

"A booth would be great," she said. She turned and held out her hand to Kieran. "Charlie, this is my friend, Kieran Quinn."

Charlie held out a hand the size of a bear's paw. "Nice to meet you, Karen," he said.

"Kieran," Maddie corrected. "It rhymes with *beer*. Now go fetch me a pitcher and a couple glasses. I'm ready to have a good time." She smiled as Charlie walked away, chuckling.

A waitress showed them to a booth and Charlie arrived a few minutes later with the beer and a basket of homemade potato chips. "You need anything, you just give me a shout. I've told everyone to just leave you in peace for a while so you can enjoy yourselves."

"I got my start right up there on that stage," Maddie said to Kieran, pointing across the dance floor.

A male singer belted out a song about drinking too much whiskey while his bandmates backed him up. The dance floor was crowded with people moving around in a slow circle. Kieran tried to imagine a younger version of Maddie up on the stage, singing a song and dreaming about fame and fortune. "It's nice that you can come back here and just chill."

"There aren't many places I can go where I feel like just a normal person, but most of the regulars here were sitting at that bar when I sang my first song on that stage."

The waitress appeared with menus and a couple glasses of water. "I just loved your last CD," she said.

"Thank you," Maddie said.

"I'm not going to trouble you now, but maybe after dinner you could sign it for me?"

"You just bring it on over and I'll do that," Maddie said. "And let anyone else know that they can do the same."

Kieran opened the menu and scanned the selections. Maddie's grandmother had fed them a huge lunch, the usual practice around Serenity Farm.

"I'm starving," she said.

He smiled to himself. He already knew her so well. He knew she'd spend at least fifteen minutes talking about the menu, discussing her choices, weighing her options before ordering at least three full meals for herself and a few for him.

"Don't you think you'd miss it?" Kieran asked. "I mean, people obviously love you. You make them happy. It must give you some satisfaction, at least."

"It does. But I'm not vain enough to believe that they would all give up listening to music tomorrow if I quit. There are plenty of other singers and bands that they can listen to. And maybe there's some young girl out there who needs a chance. Maybe they'll give her a listen."

"I just think that you shouldn't make any hard and fast decisions right now. I think you should take some time and consider what you'd be giving up."

"Ninny always told me that if what I was doing didn't make me happy, then I should quit. I started doing this not because it made me happy, but because it made my mother so happy. And I used to mistake that happiness for love. The better I sang, the more she loved me."

"And you don't think she did?"

"Oh, I'm sure she loves me, but I think she loves the business a little more. She wanted to prove something to everyone who wouldn't give her a chance. To her, it was more like revenge." Maddie looked up from the menu. "It took me a while to figure that out."

"When did you?"

"My mother was telling a story to her new assistant. The first label that offered me a recording contract was the one that turned her down. So she turned them down. I remember the night I found out. She'd told me that they didn't want me and that we'd find another label. I cried and cried. I was sure she was angry with me and that it was all my fault."

He reached out and took her hand. "I'm sorry. That must have been terrible."

"She'd forgotten my reaction to the whole thing. She was just so delighted to recount the story of how she got back at that record company to her assistant. How they'd missed out on representing a huge star because of what they did to her." Maddie took a ragged breath. "Now that I think about it, that was when I started to get stage fright."

"You realized that love had nothing to do with singing?"

She slowly nodded her head. "Yeah. I mean, I never really thought of it that way." Maddie met his gaze, her eyes growing watery. "That's it. She was my courage and when I heard the truth, I realized she wasn't in it for me." Dropping her menu, she raked her hands through her hair, then pressed her palms to her temples. "Ah, it's like a light just went on. Why didn't I realize this before?"

"Because you've never talked about it with anyone?" Kieran asked.

She sat up straight. "I have to have something to eat. Right now."

The waitress appeared a few seconds later and Maddie began the process of ordering. The young woman shot him looks of confusion as she wrote down the detailed list of dishes, but he just smiled. Then she turned to Kieran. "And for you?"

"I'm just going to finish whatever she doesn't want," Kieran said.

"Great," the waitress said. "Are y'all okay for drinks?"

Kieran nodded. "We'll be working on the beer for a while." He stared out at the dance floor and saw a few people doing the dance that Maddie had taught him the night before. "What do you say, Miss West? Why don't we have a dance before our meal gets here?"

She stood up and followed him out to the dance floor. "Do you remember what we practiced?" she asked, grinning.

Kieran pulled her into his arms. "I remember vividly. Quick, quick, slow, slow."

"Start with your left foot and…here we go. Quick, quick, slow, slow."

It was much more intimidating dancing in the midst of a crowd. He messed up a few times but as they made the second turn around the floor, he was moving much more smoothly. "Okay. I think I have this."

Maddie took his right hand in hers, turning out and holding his left hand at her waist. "All right, now we're going to do a little promenade. Same step, we're just going in the same direction now."

Maddie laughed as they made it through another

round, then stepped in front of him and twirled beneath his arm. The move surprised him and he stumbled, almost tripping over her.

The two-step segued into a slow ballad and Kieran drew her closer. His grandfather had wanted him to find a different life. Nothing could be more different that what he was experiencing right now, holding Maddie in his arms as they moved around the dance floor.

He was in love with her. At least he could admit it to himself, even if he couldn't say it out loud. When they were together, touching each other, the world seemed in perfect balance, as if nothing could tear them apart. And though these intense emotions were unfamiliar to Kieran, they felt real.

He pulled her closer, the words spinning in his head. If he was brave enough to say them, then he'd have to be brave enough to accept her reaction—good or bad. But then, maybe he should wait, until he had a better sense of how she felt. They had time. He certainly wasn't going anywhere and she didn't have plans to leave the farm anytime soon.

"This is nice," he whispered.

"It is," she said. "You're a pretty good dancer."

"I had a really good teacher."

When the song was over, they headed back to their table to find their dinner already laid out for them. But they were stopped on their way by a burly young man in a denim shirt and cowboy hat. He looked at Maddie nervously.

"I was wondering if I might ask you to dance, Miss West," he said. "They boys over there don't think you'll accept, but I told them you're too much of a lady to turn me down."

Kieran was stunned at the audacity of the guy. He and Maddie were clearly together. They were holding hands. "Listen, buddy, we're just about to have dinner and I—"

"It's all right," Maddie said. "It's just a dance. I'll be right back."

"No," Kieran said. "Our dinner is on the table." He nodded to the guy. "She'll dance with you later."

Maddie held her hand out to Kieran. "It's all right. I can dance and then I'll eat. Why don't you just sit down and wait for me. I'll be back in a few minutes." Maddie looked into his eyes. "Please?"

Kieran shook his head, then walked back to the booth, sending one last warning glare to Maddie's dance partner. He sat down and flagged down their waitress. "Double scotch on the rocks," he said.

Suddenly, he didn't feel much like eating. What the hell was she thinking, letting a complete stranger bully her into a dance? She came to the place with him. In what world did a guy not understand the code? A good man never stepped in on another guy's date.

But maybe he was in a different world. Maybe the code didn't apply in Kentucky. Kieran watched as they moved around the dance floor. The jerk was surprisingly graceful for a big guy. In fact, he put Kieran's attempts at dancing to shame.

The waitress set his drink down next to him and Kieran grabbed it and took a gulp. The scotch burned a path down his throat and his eyes began to water. "So this is what it feels like," he muttered to himself.

Jealousy. He'd never experienced the emotion before, at least not when it came to women. But then, he'd never really had so much to lose before.

If he planned to spend any time with Maddie West, country star, he was going to have to learn how to share. When she was out and about, she seemed to be public property. And there was nothing he could do about it except stand back and smile.

Falling in love had been so simple for him. He'd just followed his heart. But after tonight, Kieran had to wonder if the difficult part was still ahead— learning to ignore his ego.

MADDIE PICKED AT the slice of coconut cream pie, then pushed it aside. "I am stuffed like a Christmas goose," she said. "I am going to have to stop eating. My jeans are starting to get too tight."

"I think you look nice just the way you are," Kieran said.

Maddie stared at him for a long moment. Since she'd returned to the table, he'd been oddly silent, as if he was stewing about something. She knew he wasn't happy about her dancing with another man, but she hadn't been gone that long and the guy had been sweet and kind of nervous.

"What's wrong?" she said.

"Nothing." Kieran reached out for his drink and drained the last of it. "I'm good."

"No, you're not. I think you're angry that I danced with that guy."

Kieran shook his head. "I swear to God, I'm not angry at you."

"Then who are you angry at? Him? He's just a fan. Just a guy who's going to go home and tell all his friends that he danced with Maddie West tonight. And all his friends are going to clap him on the back and tell him how lucky he was. And then, maybe, they're going to buy a CD or a concert ticket. It's just part of the game."

"So you were nice to him because you wanted his money?"

"No, I was nice to him because it was the right thing to do. Because he probably has bought some of my CDs. And because he was nervous and sweet and I didn't want to hurt his feelings. If you think he's competition, you're—"

"That's not what I'm thinking," he said.

"Then what are you thinking?"

Their conversation was interrupted by a loud whistle from the stage. Maddie turned to find Charlie standing at the microphone, a guitar in his hand. "Ladies and gents, as you know, we've got an old friend in the house tonight. Maddie West has stopped by for a visit. Now, we don't want to put her on the spot or make her do anything she doesn't want to do, but maybe, if we put our hands together, she might give us the pleasure of a song or two. What do you say? Maddie? Will you sing for us?"

Maddie glanced over at Kieran.

"You don't have to do this," he said.

"But I think I want to."

"Are you sure?"

"Yeah," she said, without a moment of hesitation. "It's about time I sing for you, don't you think?" She set her napkin beside her plate and slowly stood, then made her way through the crowd to the stage.

To her surprise, she didn't feel that overwhelming sense of dread, the sweaty palms or the racing heartbeat. None of the symptoms that marked her stage fright in the past were affecting her now. In fact, she felt calm and composed and almost excited to get back onstage.

She climbed the steps at the side of the stage to loud applause, then took the guitar from Charlie, giving him a quick peck on the cheek. Maddie took a moment to look out at the small crowd then smiled, bending over the microphone. "How y'all doing tonight? You having fun?"

The crowd screamed their reply as she plugged the guitar into a nearby amp. She strummed the strings, then took a quick moment to tune up before she settled herself on the stool. "I don't know if y'all know this, but Charlie was one of the folks who gave me my start. My mama used to bring me here when I was fourteen years old and I'd sing my heart out and even though my songs weren't the best, everyone would clap. I'll never forget that kindness and that encouragement." She strummed the guitar again. "This is an old song, but a good one. I'm sending it out to a special friend. It's a song I used to play right here at Charlie's. It's called 'Pink Cadillac.'"

She launched into the song, her voice raspy and raw, and tinged with a bluesy sound. When she'd first started singing professionally, it had been part of her list because it was easy to play on guitar. But now, she sang it like a woman, full-grown, confident, seductive. The kind of woman that Kieran Quinn might find irresistible.

The audience sang along with the chorus and clapped during the verse, creating a raucous noise that was both thrilling and satisfying. For the first time in a very long time, she felt like she was having fun onstage. She finished the song with an aggressive guitar lick and a sexy wail and the audience erupted in wild applause.

From that moment on, Maddie didn't really think. She moved from one song to the next, talking to the audience in between, telling funny stories about her early days at Charlie's and life on the road. And when she finished up with her most recent hit, an upbeat rock song about an unfaithful boyfriend, she was certain that she'd just given the best performance of her life.

"Thank you," she called out to the audience. "Y'all have been so nice to me. Thank you."

Charlie came onstage and thanked her, then asked for another round of applause as Maddie made her way back to the table. Kieran was there and he pulled her into his arms and gave her hug. A few moments later, a crowd gathered for autographs. Maddie found a felt-tip pen and began to scribble her name on anything they presented.

By the time she finished with the last person in line, she was exhausted. She looked over at Kieran. "Let's get out of here before they talk me into singing again." She glanced around the table. "Did you take care of the check?"

"Charlie said it was on the house," Kieran replied. He held out his hand and Maddie placed her fingers in his. As they walked to the door, they nodded and smiled at the patrons, who had decided another round of applause was in order.

When they reached the parking lot, Maddie fell against him with a low groan. "I'm exhausted. I usually don't sing right after I eat because I usually throw up before the performance. But I thought it was pretty good. What do you think?"

"I thought it was amazing," Kieran said, pulling open the door of the car.

She looked up at him. "It was. And I wasn't afraid at all. Not a bit. What's that all about?"

"I don't know." He closed the door, then circled around the car and got behind the wheel.

They pulled out of the parking lot and headed toward home, the wind blowing against her damp skin. She didn't want to talk about it or try to understand why it had been so good. She just wanted to revel in a feeling that she hadn't experienced in years.

By the time they got back to the farm, Maddie felt like she'd been rung out, her limbs boneless and her mind fuzzy. Kieran parked the car in front of the house and turned it off.

"I gotta tell you, Maddie, that was one of the most incredible things I've ever seen. You had that audience so wrapped up they would have followed you off a cliff if you asked them. The way you just knew what to sing next. It was like a carnival ride."

"It felt right," she said. "And I think maybe it was because you were there."

"No," he said. "I didn't have anything to do with that."

"You gave me the courage to get back out there. To take control of my career."

"No. You had that inside you all along. You just needed a reason to make it happen." He reached out and smoothed his hand over her cheek. "You can't give that up, Maddie. You don't just walk away from a talent like yours. And as much as I'd like to steal you away from your life and keep you all to myself, that would be wrong. You need to keep performing."

"But I—"

He put his finger over her lips. "You probably need to fix things with your mother. Maybe you should get a new manager. Someone who will let you make the decisions. But you have to figure out how to make this work."

"Can't we just crawl into bed and talk about this tomorrow?" she asked.

He leaned forward and kissed her. "I think that maybe you should sleep by yourself tonight. It will give you time to make some decisions. I don't want to come between you and your career."

Maddie gasped. What was he saying? After all they'd been to each other, after all she'd told him, did he really think she couldn't make her own decisions? "Am I just supposed to forget how we feel about each other?"

"Yeah, maybe you have to. You need to think about your career first."

"And who are you to decide that for me? It's my choice. And if I choose you, that's my choice, too. Don't you dare tell me what I can and cannot feel. I've lived this career, I know what I've given up. And you don't know anything."

With that, she shoved open the car door and stepped out. "I think I *will* sleep alone tonight," she muttered. "I certainly don't want to share a bed with you."

She slammed the car door, then strode up the front porch steps. She wanted to turn around and scream at him, but Maddie was so angry she couldn't think of anything to say.

She'd thought she'd found a man who understood

her, who cared about her and what she wanted out of life. But Kieran was just like every other guy. He couldn't see past her career and her celebrity. He didn't see that all she really wanted out of life was to find someone who could love her for who she was.

Maybe she'd been wrong about him. Or maybe she never should have stepped on that stage. Maybe, maybe, maybe. The problems between them weren't going to be solved by regrets.

If he didn't love her, then it was best she found out now. Before she'd completely surrendered her heart and soul.

8

"What's wrong with him?"

Joe smoothed his hand over the back of the horse's leg. "Feel that," he said. "See how swollen that is? And it's warm. And when you touch it, he flinches. This horse used to win million-dollar races and now he can't run to the far end of the pasture. A race horse that can't race isn't much use to its owner."

"Can you fix it?" Kieran asked.

"It's been fixed before. See the scar. They've been trying to fix this horse for a long time. Thrown a lot of money at the problem. But nothing has really worked. So they decided to give up."

"What are you going to do?"

"Lots of different things," Joe said. "I know of some herbal poultices worth trying and I might put the leg in a cast. Maybe do some acupuncture. In any case, he'll need some special holistic supplements that will help renew the tendon. We'll keep him in this stall, away from the others and play some soothing music for him. And of course, that log will need icing down every day. Then, when the time is right, I'll start giving him a little exercise."

"All that? Will it work?"

"I don't know," Joe said with a shrug. "I'm willing to give it some time. I think he is, too. Because if it does work, then maybe this horse will find a good home, a place where he can be useful again. That's all a horse really wants. He just needs job to do and a person who cares for him."

Kieran straightened. "You do good work here."

"Ah, I do what I can. Sometimes it's enough. I know I couldn't do it without Maddie's help." He glanced back at Kieran. "She keeps the place going."

"She told me that."

"Horse farms, in general, are a losing proposition. You got to have money to burn in order to make one work. Maddie has given us enough that we've been able to make some nice investments, ones that will keep the farm going for a long time."

"And what if she quit singing?" he asked.

Joe slowly got to his feet, rubbing his hands on the front of his jeans. "So that's why she's come home," he murmured. "I figured something was up."

"She's having a difficult time with her mother," Kieran said. "They need to work a few things out."

"Her mother has always pushed her too hard," Joe said. "And Sarah—I mean, Maddie—has always wanted to please her. Sometimes, I think she'd be better off if she just walked away from it all, before it consumes her."

"She's so good," Kieran said.

"She is."

"If she quit, would the farm be in trouble?"

Joe shook his head. "I don't think so. We've got a fair amount of money working for us now. And there's only so many horses I can tend to. We'll do fine no matter what she decides."

"Maddie says her mother will probably show up here."

"Oh, I expect she will, just as soon as she figures out where Maddie is. And then the horse apples will hit the fan."

"It's going to be that bad?"

Joe nodded. "Oh, yeah. Maddie's mother knows exactly what buttons to push. She's kept Maddie in hand for this long. She's not about to give up now." He gave the horse a pat on the neck, then stepped out of the stall. "And speaking of my granddaughter, here she comes. I expect she's come to see you."

Kieran stepped out of the stall and pulled the door shut. Maddie gave her grandfather a hug, her gaze meeting Kieran's over Joe's shoulder. "Of course I came to see you. Ninny says lunch will be ready soon. And she wants you to go down to the cellar and fetch her some sweet pickles for the tuna salad she's making."

"Well, then, I better get hopping. Wouldn't want to keep Ninny's tuna salad waiting."

They both watched as Joe walked out of the barn, his step lively. "He's a special guy," Kieran said. "He and my grandfather would get along real well."

Maddie threw her arms around his neck and hugged him hard. "I'm sorry," she murmured. "I don't know what happened last night or why we ended up fighting, but I don't want to be mad at you. And I don't want you to be mad at me."

He nuzzled his face into the curve of her neck. "I'm not mad at you."

She stepped back. "You aren't?"

"No. I was just a little overwhelmed," he said. "I was watching a Maddie West that I didn't even know existed. I mean, I knew you were a singer. But I didn't know you were a SINGER."

"Does it make a difference?"

"Sure it does. Not in the way I feel about you. Just in the way that I think about us."

"And how is that?"

"We have a lot of things to consider Maddie. As much as I'd like to believe I could fit into your celebrity lifestyle, I'm not sure I could."

"I wouldn't expect you to. I just don't want to make any decisions right now. We can take some time and see what happens. Country music is not going to miss me if I take a few months off."

He nodded. "All right. No decisions right now."

"Except one. Maybe. I think we should go to Nashville this weekend and look at some houses for me. I need to find a place to live."

"We can do that. Have you called a real estate agent?"

Maddie nodded. "Ninny has an old friend who is an agent. She's putting together some appointments for us for tomorrow. I thought maybe we could leave this afternoon and spend the night in a hotel. I could show you a little bit of the city, maybe take you to see all the important sights."

"I think that would be fun," he said. "But I don't know if your grandfather will give me the day off."

"He has his high school boys who come on the weekend. He won't need you."

"I'm going to have to finish my work for today," he said.

"I'll help you. But let's go have some lunch first. Ninny makes the best tuna salad in the state." She wove her fingers through his and they walked through the stable. The sunny morning had given way to dark clouds and threatening rain.

Kieran felt the breeze shift and he shivered. The weather was a perfect reflection of his mood. Though he'd put on a good face for Maddie, he couldn't forget what had happened last night. Though she might want things to remain exactly as they were now, he didn't believe it was possible.

There were too many things pulling Maddie away from him, too many responsibilities, too many expectations. And what could he offer her? Seattle wasn't a hotbed of country music. And though his job skills were portable, Kieran wasn't sure he wanted to find a job in Nashville, only to sit around waiting while she went on tour. He could do that from Seattle.

Maybe the only option for them, at least right now, was a long-distance relationship. She could do what she needed to do and when she had time off, she could visit Seattle for an extended break. Or he could come to Nashville for a quick vacation. Hell, he could even meet her occasionally on the road.

If they loved each other enough, they'd find a way to work it out. He had to believe that. He couldn't accept the alternative.

"There is one thing I need to take care of before lunch," he said as they neared the stable door.

"What is that?"

He grabbed her waist and pulled Maddie into an empty stall. Then he slid the door shut. "This," he murmured, capturing her face between his hands.

His mouth met hers in a deep and demanding kiss. Maddie moaned softly as she clutched at his shirt. They stumbled until she was stopped by the wall. He grabbed her hands and pinned them above her head, deepening the kiss until she arched against him.

Desperation drove them forward and they tore at each other's clothes, searching for naked skin to touch and kiss. It was as if they had to prove to themselves that nothing had changed, that the conflicts the night before had been just a small bump in the road.

Maddie unzipped his jeans and shoved them down

over his hips. He knew what she wanted and when he picked her up and wrapped her legs around his waist, she whispered her need, urging him on.

The dress she wore bunched around her waist and her panties were pushed aside as he entered her. Kieran stopped once she sank down on top of him, gathering his control. "I don't ever want this to end," he murmured.

But he wasn't talking about the sex or even the feeling that he had when he was buried deep inside her. He didn't want this connection, this exquisite intimacy that they'd found, to suddenly stop.

They belonged together, like this, for years and years. He couldn't imagine a future that didn't include her. And though he couldn't quite figure out how it would work yet, Kieran knew he had to find a way to make it happen.

THE HOUSE WAS empty. The sound of Maddie's footsteps echoed as she wandered through the first floor. She and Kieran had already looked at three other homes in exclusive areas of Nashville, the agent explaining all the famous neighbors in each picturesque neighborhood.

But nothing had really felt right and Maddie was becoming frustrated. She didn't want to be isolated behind gates and guardhouses, hidden way from the real world. Though she knew the realities of being a celebrity, Maddie had spent the past ten years as a prisoner of her career. That had been more than enough.

Ninny's friend, Natalie, had been patient and after four failed attempts, she'd brought her to a home outside the suburbs, set on a forty-acre property near Hendersonville. The limestone farmhouse was more than a hundred years old and had been completely renovated inside and out. There was a small barn and several sheds as well as a huge orchard with a wide variety of fruit trees.

Maddie stood at the kitchen sink and stared out the window at the backyard. She could turn one of the old sheds into a recording studio. She could plant a garden and have a few horses. She could imagine a life here.

Drawing a deep breath, she continued on her tour, walking into the large addition that spanned the rear of the house. A stone fireplace dominated one wall.

It was so different than the ostentatious mansion her mother lived in. This was cozy and homey, the kind of place that would be perfect for holiday celebrations and summers outdoors. But there was one thing that she needed in this house that wasn't included in the price—Kieran.

Sooner or later they were going to have to talk about the subject they'd been so carefully avoiding. Though they acted like a couple, they were still pretending that their lives were completely independent of each other.

Maddie didn't want to believe they'd only have

six weeks together. How could they possibly build a future when their present had a beginning and an end? If she was going to buy this house, she needed to know that he would live here with her.

She heard footsteps behind her. Kieran walked over to the fireplace and slipped his arms around her waist. "What do you think?"

"It's perfect," she said. "It's like it was meant for me all along."

"I like it, too. It has a lot of character. And there's a pretty little creek running through the property."

"It's important that you like it," Maddie said. "I want this to be a place you feel comfortable."

He hugged her tight. "I think I could be comfortable here."

"I know we haven't talked about the future or what's going to happen when it's time for you to go home. But you need to know that I want you to be a part of my life. I'm not really sure how that will work, but—"

"I want the same thing, Maddie."

She looked up at him. "You do?"

"Yes."

A rush of relief washed over her. Tears pressed at the corners of her eyes and she laughed, the emotion getting the better of her. "I—I wasn't sure. We haven't known each other that long, but I know what I want. I want us to be together."

"We'll figure it out," he said.

"We will. I know we can."

Maddie pushed up on her toes and kissed him, wrapping her arms around his neck and pressing her body to his. "Did you look at the bedrooms? There's a fireplace in the master one. And a very big bathtub."

"That might be fun," he said. "Should we get rid of the agent and give it a try?"

"No! We can't use the bathtub until I buy the house." Maddie ran her fingers through her hair. "I can't believe I'm going to buy a house. I feel like such an adult." She hurried over to the stove and ran her hands along the edge. "I'm going to have my own appliances. My own wine refrigerator."

"So, what do you think?" the agent said as she walked into the kitchen.

"I love it," Maddie said. "So how do we do this? Do I just get a check or do we give them cash? I don't even know how much it costs. Not that it really matters. As long as it doesn't cost more than I have. But then, I'm not even sure how much I have."

"I think she wants to make an offer," Kieran said.

"Not an offer," Maddie said. "I want to buy it."

"First, Natalie will write up an offer," Kieran explained. "You'll decide how much you want to pay for the property. You can go with the asking price, or you could offer something lower."

"No, I'll pay what they want," Maddie said.

"I think the house is a bit overpriced," Natalie said. "I'd recommend going in about five percent below the asking price. That would put you right at market value. And I think they'd probably take it. I'm sure you won't have to worry about financing."

"I have some money put aside, but not enough to cover the whole cost," Maddie said. "It may take some convincing to get the rest from my mother. Even though it is my money, she manages it."

"Well, why don't you do a twenty percent down payment and we'll get you approved for financing on the rest? I know a banker who would be happy to have your business."

"Good. Now that we have that figured out, let's just give them what they want. Then I'll be happy and they'll be happy."

"But I won't," Kieran said. "Let Natalie do her job. You want the sale to be contingent on an inspection and an appraisal. That you can afford."

"All right. I'm going to listen to you both. I want this house and if you do anything to mess it up, I'm never going to forgive you. Just write up this offer and I'll sign it and then—well, we'll do whatever is supposed to come next."

Natalie wrote up the offer and gave it to Maddie. "Should I sign it?"

"It's up to you," Kieran said. "If this is your house, then sign it. If you have any doubts, we'll keep looking."

"It's my house," she said. She signed her legal name, Sarah M. Westerfield, then quickly dated it. "All right."

They walked out of the house a half hour later,

after Maddie had walked through it just one more time. The weather had turned rainy and Maddie was glad Kieran had thought to put the top of the Caddy up. She got inside and waited for him. When he got in, she looked over at him.

"This, being an adult, is kind of scary."

"I was really nervous when I bought my place," he said. "And I didn't have the kind of money you do."

"I feel kind of nauseated."

"That's because we haven't had lunch yet. Let's go back to the hotel, order room service and spend the rest of the day watching movies."

"That sounds like a really good idea. And after that, we'll go downtown and listen to some music."

As they drove back to Nashville, Maddie thought about everything they'd talked about. At least now, she knew where she stood. They both wanted to continue and were both headed in the same direction.

After all that had happened over the past week and a half, she'd never expected to end up here, buying a house, planning a life for herself. But with every day that passed, she was more determined to strike out on her own.

She'd fire her mother as her manager and find someone who would understand the new path she wanted to take. Her mother was an excellent manager. There were any number of singers and songwriters in Nashville who would jump at the chance to work with her.

Then Maddie would start talking to friends, finding artists who might want to collaborate with her. She'd dust off some of the songs she'd written years ago and offer them to young singers on the verge of breaking out. Making a living as a songwriter wouldn't be a difficult transition.

It would all work. Just like Kieran said. "I'm really happy," Maddie murmured. "A few weeks ago, I was so miserable and now I'm really happy."

Kieran said. "And all because of a turkey sandwich."

"What?"

"That's what you bought me that morning in the bus station. A turkey sandwich. A sub, actually. If you'd been in front of me in line, we never would have met."

"I guess we were pretty lucky, weren't we? I'm thinking I'll buy you another sandwich. And maybe I'll get lucky tonight."

"You don't need to feed me to get lucky," he teased. "In fact, I need to stop eating all your leftovers. My jeans are starting to get a little tight."

"Then we'll skip lunch and dinner and just begin our next exercise plan."

"And what is that?" Kieran asked.

"Sex. Sex. And more sex," Maddie said. "Hours and hours of hot, sweaty sex."

"That's a diet that I'm going to enjoy."

KIERAN NOTICED THE wary look on Maddie's face the moment he pulled the Cadillac to a stop in front of her grandparents' house.

"Oh, no," she murmured, staring at a slender figure standing on the porch.

"What wrong?"

"It's my mother," she said. "Keep driving. Just go. Now, before she has a chance to get into her car."

Though Kieran was tempted to follow her orders, he knew Maddie was ready to face her mother. She'd made an offer on a house for herself, met with some songwriter friends in Nashville, interviewed a new manager, and decided she wanted him in her future. The only thing she had left to do was to conquer her fear of her mother.

"You're going to be fine," Kieran said. He got out of the car then jogged around to open her door. "I'll be in the stable if you need me."

"No," Maddie said.

"No?"

She grabbed the car keys from his hand, then jumped back into the car, locking the door behind her. An instant later, the engine roared to life and Maddie threw the car into gear. It swerved around the circle drive and headed down the driveway.

Maddie's mother hurried down the front steps. "Maddie! Maddie, come back here."

"I don't think she can hear you," Kieran said.

She leveled an annoyed gaze at him. "She doesn't drive."

"She does now. Although she's driving without a license. But I don't think she's going very far."

"Who are you?"

Kieran held out his hand. "Kieran Quinn. I guess you could say I'm your daughter's boyfriend?"

"Oh. You're the one." She shook her head. "I should have known. You are exactly the kind of boy she can't resist."

"I hope I'm the one," Kieran said. "Because as far as I'm concerned, Maddie is the one for me."

She took a step forward, her eyebrow arched in a condescending smirk. "Really? The last thing my daughter needs is the drama of some silly romance. Sure, you may have come to her rescue like some fairy-tale prince, but Maddie knows what she has to do. She knows where she belongs."

"Then you shouldn't have anything to worry about," he said. "She'll decide for herself."

"If you haven't brainwashed her with your pretty blue eyes and your devastating smile."

"I do my best," Kieran said.

"All right, let's just get down to business. How much do you want?"

Kieran laughed. "I don't want anything—except Maddie's happiness."

"Don't be ridiculous. Everyone has a price. I should warn you that Maddie's relationships never last more than a month. Sooner or later, she'll grow bored and you'll be left wondering what you did wrong. If you take my offer right now, you won't walk away empty-handed." She reached into her designer bag and withdrew her checkbook. "How do you spell your first name?"

The sound of an approaching car caught their attention and Kieran watched as the Cadillac came roaring back up the driveway. Maddie slammed on the brakes, then jumped out of the car. But she'd forgotten to put it in Park and it began to move. With a tiny scream, she jumped back behind the wheel and turned off the ignition.

As Maddie approached her mother, Kieran could see the anger in her eyes. "I'm not going back," she said. "I don't care what you've come to say to me. It's not going to work. Just go home, Mama."

"Maddie, stop this. You have no idea what you're saying. You have obligations and responsibilities. Advances have been paid. If you don't do the work, you'll be in breach of contract and they'll take you to court."

"Then give the advances back," Maddie said.

"I can't. They've already been spent."

Maddie frowned. "What do you mean?"

"You have business expenses. The economy hasn't been that great. The tour didn't make as much as we thought it would."

"What about record sales?" she said. "My last album was number one for seven weeks."

"You know we don't make a lot on record sales. The money is in touring and publishing. And maybe I haven't spent a lot of time marketing your catalog, but that's my fault. I'm going to do a better job with that in the future."

"So how bad is it, Mama? Are you saying that I don't have any choice in the matter?"

"We have obligations," her mother murmured.

"You have obligations. Like that ridiculous house you bought. How much is that costing us?"

"We're going to have to move," Constance said.

"Not me. I bought a home for myself."

"What? You bought a house?"

"Yes, Mama. I wanted a place of my own. I thought I deserved a place of my own—a life of my own—after living out your dreams for the past ten years."

"They were your dreams, too," she said.

"Yes, they were. But now I have my own plans."

Constance threw up her hands and began to pace back and forth in front of Maddie. "I suppose this— this person is behind your sudden rebellion? You'd listen to him before you'd listen to me."

"I trust Kieran," Maddie said.

"You've only known him for a week!" Constance protested. "I gave birth to you." She stopped pacing, then took a moment to compose herself. "This is a business matter, Maddie. I think we should sit down and work this out."

"No," Maddie said. "I want Kieran here." She strode to his side and grabbed his hand. "I love him. And he loves me—I think. Anything you have to say to me you can say to him."

Kieran gave her hand a squeeze, then bent close to

whisper in her ear. "You can do this on your own," he said. "You can, Maddie."

"But I need—"

"You don't need anyone. You'll make the right choice. I know you will." He brushed his lips across hers. "And I do love you."

Her expression brightened. "You do?"

Kieran wanted to pull her into his arms and kiss her until she couldn't catch her breath. But he knew that now was not the time. "I do. I'm just going to head out to the stables and catch up on my work. When you're finished here, come and get me?"

Maddie nodded. She cupped his face in her hands and kissed him again, softly and sweetly, her tongue teasing at his. "I love you," she said with a smile. "I love saying that. I love you."

Kieran stole another quick kiss, then glanced over at Constance West. "Miss West, it was a pleasure meeting you. I suspect we'll be seeing a lot of each other in the future."

Constance scoffed, crossing her arms over her chest. "I wouldn't count on it," she said.

Kieran walked away, glancing back once at Maddie and giving her an encouraging smile. This was her fight, her time to take control. If she couldn't stand up for herself, then he'd never have a place in her life anyway. Playing second fiddle to her mother would be an untenable existence. But if she could break away, then they had a chance. After all, she loved him.

Kieran smiled to himself. After worrying over the words, not to mention when and if he'd say them, they'd just come out, as if the declaration had been made a hundred times before.

"I love her," he murmured. "I love her."

He knew it was true. There wasn't a doubt in his mind. And though he wasn't so sure about their future together, Kieran was certain that his feelings would never change.

He found Joe in the barn, bent over a table, mixing one of his special poultices. "Hey," Kieran said as he approached.

Joe glanced over at him and chuckled. "You're still alive. I take that as a good sign."

"When did she get here?"

"Last night. I tried to convince her that we hadn't seen Maddie, but Sarah wouldn't lie. She's our daughter and though we don't agree with some of her choices, we still love her."

"How much do you know about Maddie's finances?"

"Not much beyond what she gives us for the farm. Her mother keeps that information to herself. I know Maddie isn't really aware of what she has."

Kieran nodded. "This is not going to turn out well," he said.

"Then I reckon you're going to have to do something about that," Joe said.

"I don't know if I can," he said.

"Do you love my granddaughter?"

Kieran nodded. "I do. It surprises the hell out of me because I never thought I'd make that particular leap. Especially not after just a week or two. But I can't seem to help myself."

"Yeah? Welcome to the family. From the moment that baby girl came into my life, she's had me twisted around her little finger. It's hard not to love her."

"I'm just beginning to realize that," Kieran said. "So, I'm pretty much a lost cause? Is that what you're telling me?"

Joe clapped him on the shoulder. "Yep. That would be the long and short of it. But look at it this way. She will make your life more interesting than you ever imagined. Every day will be an adventure."

"Should I worry?" Kieran asked.

Joe shook his head. "Naw. Maddie takes after her grandmother. I've never regretted making that woman my wife. I never know what she's going to say or do. But whatever it is, it will make me smile. And that's the secret to a very long and happy life. You have to spend a lot of time smiling."

Kieran chuckled. If that was all it took to live to a ripe old age, then Maddie was definitely the woman for him. Because when he thought about her, he couldn't keep the sappy grin off his face.

9

"YOUR MOTHER IS telling the truth," Kieran said. His gaze met hers and Maddie could see the anguish in his eyes. Though she didn't want to hear what he had to say, she knew it would be much easier to take coming from him.

She'd asked him to look over the accounting from every facet of her career, from her record contracts to her concert appearances to publishing rights. Her mother had reluctantly sent boxes of files, stuffed with reams of paper.

They sat on the bed in his room, surrounded by stacks of reports and documents. He'd been pouring over them for the past three days, making notes and promising that he'd get to the bottom of her financial problems.

"You're sure?"

Kieran nodded. "She may not have been a great business manager, but at least she never fixed the books. It's all right here in black and white." He looked down at the papers. "From what I can see, it's the tours that brought you down. It started about five years ago. She seriously overspent on one particular tour and has been trying to make it up ever since, throwing good money after bad."

"Why didn't she say something?"

"I guess she was gambling that she'd be able to make it up on the next tour."

He pulled out a spreadsheet comparing the expenses and incomes from her last five tours. Maddie looked at it, but the columns of numbers just blurred together. She didn't need to see the figures to know that she was in deep trouble. Kieran's mood was enough to tell her that.

"You might want to get someone to audit the concert production company," he suggested. "Just to make sure they weren't taking advantage of your mother's rather questionable business sense. Some of these expenses seemed to go up sharply from one tour to the next."

"This is my fault," Maddie said, burying her face in her hands. "I have no one to blame but myself."

"No," Kieran said. He took her hand and pressed his lips to her wrist. "You trusted her. She is your mother."

"But I knew she was overspending. There were times that we had all the cash in the world and then all of a sudden, she'd go on this austerity kick where she wouldn't spend a dime. She'd order a new roomful of furniture for her house and the next day she'd cancel it."

"You probably would have been more interested if you hadn't gotten into the business at such an early age. What fourteen-year-old is going to understand all this?"

"I'm twenty-four," Maddie said. "I could have made a better effort." She sighed. "So, now that you've told me the bad news, what's the really bad news?"

"You're not going to be able to buy the house. Luckily, we've been sitting on the counter-offer for a few days. You can just turn it down and you'll be out of that deal, no money lost. Your mother's house, on the other hand, is mortgaged to the hilt. She's completely underwater."

"Underwater? What does that mean?"

"The house is worth less than the outstanding mortgage. When the economy went bad, housing prices dropped, so she basically overpaid for the house. Without income, she won't be able to keep it, but she probably can't sell it for enough to pay off the amount outstanding. So she'll have to carry a considerable amount of debt."

Maddie buried her face again. "This is just getting worse and worse. If I replace her as my manager, she'll lose the house. She loves that place. She'll never forgive me."

"She'll probably lose it anyway, Maddie."

Maddie shook her head. "No. I can make another

new record and go back out on the road. I can tour for a few more years. I'll do smaller venues. We'll cut back on travel. I'll get a bus instead of flying on a private jet. I'll take away all her credit cards and put her on a budget."

"I thought you didn't want to tour," he said softly.

"I—I don't really have much choice. That's where the money is," Maddie said, crawling off the bed. She paced the length of the room, back and forth, the distraction helping her think. "I'll get a new manager. I'll pay off my mother's mortgage as soon as I can and give her time to get on her feet. And I'll make sure there's enough for the farm. If I work really hard, I can do it."

"And what about you?" Kieran asked.

"What I want can wait," she murmured. She knew what she was saying, what she was asking of him. They'd have to put their future on hold if she wanted to clean up the mess her mother had made. She swallowed hard, knowing what she was about to say could change her life forever. "You don't have to wait," she murmured.

"What?"

She risked a glance up at him. "You don't have to wait. I'll understand if you want to move on. The next few years are going to be crazy. And I'll be so busy that—"

"Stop," Kieran said, grabbing her hand. He pulled her back onto the bed. "Don't say anything else."

"I have to say it," Maddie murmured, sitting on

her heels. "It's not that I don't love you, because I do. But this is my family. I have to take care of them first."

She crawled over the papers and curled up next to him, nestling into the curve of his arm. "Please tell me you understand."

"I do," Kieran said. "But that doesn't mean I'm going to forget about us."

"I think maybe you should," Maddie said. "At least for the short-term. When it's time for you to go home, you should go. You should live your life as if you'd never met me. And when I straighten everything out, I'll come to Seattle and we'll start again—if you're still interested."

"Maddie, we can make this work now. It's only a couple years. I'll come to see you. We'll meet up on the road. When you've got a few days off, you can come and visit me."

"I want that," Maddie said. "But I know how difficult it is. I've tried before, with men who understood the demands of celebrity. And it never worked."

"It *will* work."

"All right," Maddie said. "But you have to promise me something. If you ever want out, if it ever becomes too much, you'll tell me. I won't try to convince you to change your mind. We'll just say goodbye and that will be the end of it."

"I'm not going to stop loving you," he said.

"No regrets, no tears. It will just be done and we'll go on with our lives. Promise me that."

"All right," Kieran said. "I promise."

"Now, you can make love to me."

Maddie pushed up onto her knees and pulled her dress over her head. She wore nothing beneath, knowing that their evening would come to this. Kieran's gaze slowly drifted over her body. Like a caress, it sent a shiver skittering over her skin. He reached out and cupped her breast in his hand, then slipped his arms around her waist and pulled her close.

His head rested on her breasts and Maddie ran her fingers through his thick, dark hair. The thought of being separated from him brought a deep ache to her heart. How would she ever deal with the loss, the empty spot beside her in her bed?

Maddie pulled back, then slowly pushed the piles of paper to the floor. When the bed was cleared, she drew Kieran to his knees and undressed him, her fingertips and lips teasing at his bare skin.

When he was finally naked, she pulled him down on top of her, writhing beneath him until he was deep inside her. For a long time, neither one of them moved. The seduction was limited to a long, deep kiss.

And then, he drew back and plunged deep, the wild sensation of him filling her causing her to cry out in surprise. His rhythm was slow and gentle at first, but as Maddie felt herself reaching for her release, he grew more determined, more desperate.

She whispered his name, whispered her needs,

telling him how much she wanted him. And when she finally felt her orgasm overwhelm her, he was there, his shudders and spasms melding with hers.

It was always this way, Maddie thought to herself. As if they'd just discovered this new way to touch each other. Every doubt she had, every worry, dissolved in the midst of their passion. She laid her head on his chest and listened to his heartbeat as it gradually slowed to a normal rhythm.

There would be nights, sleepless nights, where she would want to remember every sensation, every exquisite moment they spent together. She closed her eyes and committed this night to memory, burning the details indelibly in her brain.

Was he right? Would they be able to survive the time apart? Or was he merely telling her what she wanted to hear? She would know soon enough.

THE WIPERS OF Kieran's SUV slapped back and forth, brushing aside the wet snow that fell from the November sky. He glanced down at the clock. He and Dermot had left Seattle early that morning, their skis packed in the back, the CD changer loaded with enough tunes to get them through the eight-hour drive.

They were just twenty miles from their destination, but the snow was now sticking to the road now and it was becoming more slippery with every mile that passed.

"I don't understand why we had to drive," Dermot said. "It's kind of a waste of time."

"We haven't seen much of each other lately," Kieran said. "I thought it would give us a chance to talk."

"If you wanted to talk, we could have had lunch. Or gone out for a beer. Or sat next to each other on the plane. We wouldn't have had to drive to—" Dermot paused. "Where the hell are we going?"

"Missoula," Kieran said.

"Montana? What kind of skiing is there in Missoula? I thought we were going to Idaho."

"No. Missoula. And we're not going skiing."

Dermot twisted around in the passenger seat. "What? What do you mean we're not going skiing? I brought my gear."

"I had to tell you that or you probably wouldn't have come along."

"Why? What are we going to do?"

Kieran took a deep breath. "We're going to see a concert. A singer named Maddie West is playing in Missoula tonight. She's…a friend of mine."

"Maddie West? I've never heard of her."

"That's because you don't listen to country music."

"And you do?" Dermot asked.

"Yeah. I listen to her. I have all her CDs." He reached into the glove box and pulled out the cases, handing them to Dermot.

Dermot reached up and turned on the light above the mirror. "She's a kid," he said.

"Not anymore. She made those when she was young. She's twenty-four now."

"And how did you meet this girl—woman?"

"The same way you met Rachel. On our little six-week sojourn. I picked her up in the bus station in Denver the day after I left Seattle. And we were together for the next two weeks. Then she had to leave to record her new album. And now, she's doing another concert tour. I haven't seen her since early September."

"You haven't seen her for almost three months and you brought me along?"

"She doesn't know I'm coming. And if I don't see her, or she refuses to see me, I'm going to get thoroughly drunk. Then I'll need you to drive me home."

"Why haven't you said anything about this girl?" Dermot asked. "We've all talked about our time away and all you've mentioned is old race horses."

"I didn't want to get into it." Kieran glanced over at his brother. "I'm not really sure what *it* is right now. We talk, we Skype. We keep planning to meet up, but something always gets in the way. I guess I just want to see where we stand."

"It's only been a couple of months," Dermot said.

"You don't know how long a couple of months feels without her."

Dermot chuckled. "Oh, I think I have a pretty good idea. So, what's the plan? Do we have tickets?

Are you going stand in the audience and wave at her until she sees you? Are you going to try to jump on the stage?"

"I don't have tickets. I figured we can pick some up from scalpers if we have to. But I'm going to go to the stage door and try to talk myself in. If I can get a message to her, she'll come out and talk to me."

Dermot groaned. "This all seems just a little pathetic. They're going to think you're some crazed fan."

"Do I look like a crazed fan?" Kieran asked.

"No. You look like a lovesick fool."

Kieran pulled the car off the interstate. "Well, maybe I do. I am a lovesick fool and I'm not ashamed to admit it. This woman is just...everything. She's funny and talented and crazy and beautiful. And I want to spend every minute of every day with her."

"And you expect her to give up her big career and come live with you in Seattle?"

Kieran shook his head. "No. I'm not sure what we're going to do. I really don't care at this point. I'd be willing to go wherever she wanted as long as we're together."

A long silence grew between the brothers as Kieran navigated through the streets of Missoula. When Kieran spotted the theater, he followed the signs to a nearby parking garage and parked the SUV.

"What am I supposed to do?" Dermot asked.

"Come with me. I might need you to run interference."

He grinned. "Now, that sounds like fun."

Winter had already come to Missoula. Snow coated the streets and sidewalks. He wondered where Maddie was staying, if she'd spend the night in Missoula or leave that night. He noticed a huge bus with tinted windows parked outside the stage door.

"Look," Kieran said. "She's probably in there." He ran across the street, Dermot following him. When they reached the bus, he knocked politely on the door. But it didn't open.

"Now what?" Dermot asked.

Kieran ran along the side of the bus. "Maddie West! Maddie!"

Dermot joined him and a bunch of fans hanging around the sidewalk began to shout and clap. A few minutes later the door opened and a sleepy bus driver emerged. "She's not on the bus," he said. "She's inside. Now bug off."

The crowd dispersed, mumbling to themselves. But Kieran wasn't deterred. "Stage door," he said.

They found the entrance not far from where the bus was parked. He waited until someone came out before he slipped inside, motioning Dermot along with him.

A security guard sat at a desk in a small lobby, a locked door still blocking the way to the stage. "Can I help you?" he asked.

"I'm here to see Maddie West. My name is Kieran Quinn." He cleared his throat. "She's expecting me."

He picked up a clipboard. "You're not on the list. Sorry. You're going to have to wait outside."

Dermot stepped up to the desk. "Listen, the guy has driven all the way from Seattle to see this woman. Can't you just let him say hello? He'll only be a few seconds. They know each other."

"Sorry, buddy. Unless you're on the list, I can't let you in."

"A note," Kieran said. "Can you take her a note?"

"I don't bother the performers. If I did, I'd lose my job."

"All right," Kieran said. "How about if I give you a note for her mother. Constance West. She's about five-six, with short blond hair. She wears a lot of jewelry, a lot of rings. And red lipstick."

The guard frowned. "Yeah. I know her." He thought about the request for a few seconds, then handed Kieran a notepad. "I'll try."

Kieran quickly scribbled a short message, then handed it to the security guard. The man went to the door, then punched in a code. A few seconds later he came back. "I gave it to one of the stage managers," he said. "They'll get it to Ms. West. Why don't you just have a seat?"

While they waited, more fans attempted to get backstage but were sent off without success. Three huge bouquets of flowers arrived along with a fruit basket and those were dutifully taken backstage.

Kieran was almost ready to give up when the door opened and Constance West poked her head out. She motioned him to follow her. Dermot walked behind him through the door and they followed her into the dark backstage area.

"I'd like to talk to Maddie," Kieran said.

She turned on them both, her gaze shifting between the two of them in confusion. "I'm going to tell you this just once and then I'm going to ask that you leave. Any expectations that you have about my daughter are foolish at best. She's committed herself to her career and she just doesn't have time for a personal life. I know exactly why you're attracted to her, but don't think that you can influence her in any way against me. I think we proved that point back at her grandparents' place. I will tell her that you stopped by after the show. If she'd like to see you then, she'll find you." She turned and nodded at a security guard and he stepped up to show them out.

Kieran glanced over at Dermot. "Come on. Let's go."

"You're just going to give up?"

"No," Kieran said. "You occupy her mother. I'm going to sneak past her. Go, now."

They turned back from the door, Kieran veering away from the security guard and Dermot heading back to Maddie's mother. Kieran grabbed a vase of flowers from a passing stagehand and hid behind them as he watched the guard go after his twin brother.

He quickly moved away from the door and when he saw a musician, he stopped. "I have to get these to Maddie," he said. "Would you know where she is?"

The musician pointed to the other side of the stage and Kieran looked across the empty area to see Maddie arranging her guitars on a rack. He glanced around, then headed toward her. "Maddie!"

She looked up and her eyes went wide. A smile broke out across her face and she ran out to meet him midstage. "Oh, my God. You're here. What are you doing here?"

"I decided to come and see you."

"Are those for me?"

"Yes," he said, handing her the flowers.

She wasn't sure what to do with them, but then he took the vase back and set it on the drum riser. "You look beautiful."

She threw her arms around his neck and kissed him. All the distance and the time that had passed between them dissolved in that instant. Kieran picked her up off her feet, losing himself in the sweet taste of her mouth.

He drew back to see her eyes fill with tears. Maddie touched his face. "I've missed you so much. I know we talk all the time, but I've missed touching you. And being with you."

"Are you staying in town tonight?"

"No," Maddie said. "We have to leave right after the show. We're due in Sacramento tomorrow. Now that we have the bus, the schedule is more complicated."

"You look tired," he said.

She nodded. "I'm fine."

"There he is!"

The sound of Constance West's voice echoed over the empty stage. A few seconds later a trio of security staff rushed across the stage and grabbed Kieran's arms.

"Stop!" Maddie said. "Take your hands off him. He's with me."

"Get him out of here," Constance said.

"No," Maddie said. She pushed at the security guards and they finally let him go.

"Maddie, you have a show to prepare for. Now is not the time for guests," Constance said. "You need to focus on what's important."

She turned to her mother. "Leave us," she said. "Just go." The guards and Constance refused to move. "Go!" she screamed. "Or I'll walk out of this theater right now."

They finally did as she asked and Kieran watched as they walked away, only to take a post on the other side of the stage.

"I can't do this," she whispered. "I can't see you for just a few hours and then let you go. It hurts too much."

"Maddie, I—"

She pressed a finger to his lips and shook her head. "No. You have to go. When this is all finished and I'm free of these obligations, then we can think about us." She took a ragged breath. "Kiss me," she said. "And then say goodbye."

Kieran bent close and touched his lips to hers. A single tear fell onto her cheek and he brushed it away with his thumb. "I love you," he said.

"I love you."

He took a step back and then another. It took all his willpower to walk away, but he knew that if he stayed any longer, it would be impossible for him to leave at all. Though he was prepared to give up everything for her, she hadn't reached that point yet. He'd give her the time she needed.

"Bye, Maddie," he said.

"Bye, Kieran."

He turned and didn't look back. The urge to run back and grab her, to carry her away with him, was too overwhelming.

He found Dermot waiting outside the stage door. "Did you find her?"

"Yeah," Kieran said, striding down the sidewalk toward the parking lot. "I did."

"Well, what happened?"

"I kissed her and told her I loved her."

"And?"

"And nothing. That's all I came to do."

Dermot stopped, then cursed. "We drove all this way for that? You're not going to stick around until after the show?"

"No," Kieran said. "This is enough for now. There'll be another time."

"The road back here is awful narrow, Miss West. I'm not sure there will be a place to turn around."

Maddie stared out the front window of the bus. "It's a boatyard," she said. "They must have trucks coming back here all the time. I think you'll be okay."

Maddie felt a flutter of excitement in her stomach. They'd driven all the way from Phoenix, just Maddie and Ben, the bus driver. Now that they'd arrived, they'd park the bus somewhere in Seattle and she'd send Ben home on a flight so that he could spend Christmas with his family.

She had two glorious weeks with absolutely no commitments. And she intended to spend them in Seattle with Kieran.

It had been over a month since she'd seen him last, a month since she'd watched him walk away from her. Sending him away had been the most difficult thing she'd ever done, beyond leaving him for the first time. The pressures on her were almost unbearable and the moment she'd seen him, she was ready to run away, to toss aside all her responsibilities and leave with him.

So she'd done the only thing she could do—she sent him away, while she still could. Since that night, Maddie hadn't stopped thinking about him. Living her life on the road had been exhausting.

They were playing smaller venues, the band was

smaller, the accommodations were smaller. But cutting back had made them much more profitable. She'd almost made enough to pay off her mother's house.

After the New Year, she'd go back to Nashville to finish the CD she'd begun in L.A. in September. And then she had three months of touring before she was due to leave for Japan and Australia. After that, there were no more obligations, nor any more outstanding debts.

"Here we are," Ben said. "Quinn Yachtworks."

Maddie stared out the window at the waterfront property. Sailboats, their masts stabbing into the gray sky, were scattered around the spacious yard. A small gate allowed access to the lot and to the buildings beyond. "Do you see a sign for the offices?" she asked.

"Looks like they're over there," Ben said, pointing to a brick building. "That one's got windows."

Maddie drew a deep breath, then smoothed her hands over the front of her jacket. "All right. Find a place to park the bus and then get yourself to the airport. I want you home with your family for Christmas eve, do you understand?"

Ben nodded. "Are you sure you're going to be all right?"

"Of course I am," Maddie said. She grabbed her bag from a nearby seat, then picked up her guitar and stood at the door. "I'll see you in the New Year."

She ran through the lot, dodging puddles while raindrops splattered on her face. By the time she reached the office door, her hair was wet and stringy. She pushed open the door and walked inside. To her surprise, she didn't find a reception area. Instead she walked into a huge room filled with wide tables. Blueprints were lying everywhere, along with wooden models of sailboat hulls.

Maddie set her things down on the floor and then slowly wandered along the wall, looking at photographs of huge sailboats, cutting through blue water. This was his world, Maddie thought to herself. A world she knew nothing about.

She pressed her hand to her racing heart. She felt as if she was meeting a stranger. How would he react to her surprise? They'd only spoken a few times over the past three weeks and each time she'd felt a distance growing between them. She knew he was trying to make things easier on her, but in fact, she'd only felt worse.

"Let me just grab the plans."

The voice was so familiar. Maddie held her breath and a moment later, Kieran walked into the room. He froze when he saw her. A hesitant smile curled the corners of his mouth. "Hi," he said.

"Hi," Maddie replied.

She crossed the room in a matter of seconds, throwing herself into his arms and kissing him. But his reaction was cold and dispassionate. Maddie stepped back and looked up into his face, stunned that things had changed so profoundly between them.

"Are you Maddie?" he asked.

"Kieran, what's wrong? Are you angry at me?"

He cleared his throat. "I'm quite sure Kieran is not angry with you. I think Kieran is going to be thrilled to see you. Unfortunately, I'm not Kieran. I'm Dermot."

Maddie gasped. "Oh, my God. I'm so sorry." She shook her head. "Of course you are."

"We do look a bit different."

"I guess I was just so excited to see you. I mean, Kieran. And I forgot all about you. Dermot. Kieran's twin…" She held out her hand. "It's a pleasure to meet you. I'm Maddie."

"Yes." He shook her hand. "I can see that."

"Is Kieran here?"

"He is."

At that moment, a shout echoed from somewhere outside the room. "Dermot, bring the Welling plans, too."

"Get them yourself," Dermot called.

"Jaysus, what is your problem. Just pick them up and—"

Dermot winked at Maddie. "I can't find them."

A few seconds later, Kieran stormed into the room. He was dressed in a suit and tie, his shaggy hair neatly combed. He froze when he saw Maddie.

Dermot chuckled. "He's the one you're supposed to kiss." He walked over to Kieran and clapped him on the shoulder. "I'll call Welling and move our meeting to tomorrow. I'm sure you have better things to do today."

Kieran grinned. "I'm sure I do."

When they were alone, Maddie slowly approached him. She brushed her wet hair out of her eyes, her gaze fixed on him. "So, I was in the area and I thought I'd stop in and say hi."

He grabbed her waist and pulled her into his arms, his mouth coming down on hers. The kiss took her breath away and she melted against him, a flood of desire racing through her. It was everything that she'd remembered it to be. The attraction hadn't faded. Every nerve in her body suddenly came alive, every thought in her head was focused on him.

"Tell me how much time we have. Are you on your way to another concert?"

"No. I'm here to stay. For the holidays. Two weeks, if you'll have me."

Kieran laughed. "If I'll have you? Of course I'll have you. I can't think of anything I'd rather have for Christmas than you."

"Good," she said. "I have an early Christmas gift for you." She walked back to the spot where her guitar case sat and opened it, then pulled out the Maddie West calendar. She held it out to him and Kieran took it from her.

"It's you," he said.

"I've written all my dates in there. You and I are going to sit down and figure out exactly how we're going to make this work over the next six months. And then, after that, we're going to figure out how were going to make the rest of our lives work. Together."

"I have something for you," he said. "I didn't think I was going to see you for the holidays. Should I save it for Christmas?"

She shook her head. "You know me. I prefer instant gratification. I can't wait."

"I've been carrying it around for a couple of weeks. Trying to figure out how to frame my question." He reached into the breast pocket of his jacket and pulled out a small ring box. Kieran flipped it open to reveal a beautiful emerald in a vintage setting.

Maddie's breath caught in her throat as he took it out of the box and slipped it on her finger.

"I don't know what kind of ring this is. If you want it to be an engagement ring, I'll get down on my knee right now and ask you to marry me. And if you want to wait, then this is a promise to you. That we will have a future together. And if that's too much for now, then it's just a gift, a token of my love and affection." He drew a deep breath. "I love you, Maddie. And I promise that I'll do everything in my power to make you happy. For the rest of your life."

Maddie looked down at the ring. "I love you, Kieran. And that's the only promise I need."

He hooked his finger beneath her chin and drew her into a gentle kiss. "You are all I've ever wanted."

"And you are everything I've ever needed." She

threw her arms around his neck and gave him a fierce hug. "My mother is going to pitch a fit."

"I can imagine."

"And the tabloids are going to go crazy."

"I expected that."

"But I don't care," Maddie said. "Nothing is going to change how I feel about you."

As he kissed her again, Maddie lost herself in the pure joy she found in his arms. Her life had finally become her own and yet, it was theirs, too. She could picture herself marrying him, starting a family, growing old together. Everything that made for a happy life was here, with Kieran.

She'd have to write a song about it. After all, every great love story deserved a song.

* * * * *

COMING NEXT MONTH from Harlequin® Blaze™
AVAILABLE SEPTEMBER 18, 2012

#711 BLAZING BEDTIME STORIES, VOLUME IX
Bedtime Stories
Rhonda Nelson and Karen Foley
Two of Harlequin Blaze's bestselling authors invite you to curl up in bed with their latest collection of sensual fairy tales, guaranteed to inspire sweet—and *very* sexy—dreams!

#712 THE MIGHTY QUINNS: CAMERON
The Mighty Quinns
Kate Hoffmann
Neither Cameron Quinn nor FBI agent Sophie Reyes is happy hanging out in Vulture Creek, New Mexico. But when Cameron helps Sophie on a high profile case, he realizes that sexy Sophie has stolen his heart.

#713 OWN THE NIGHT
Made in Montana
Debbi Rawlins
Jaded New Yorker Alana Richardson wants to go a little country with Blackfoot Falls sheriff Noah Calder. He just needs to figure out if she belongs in his bed...or in jail!

#714 FEELS SO RIGHT
Friends With Benefits
Isabel Sharpe
Physical therapist Demi Anderson knows she has the right job when the world's sexiest man walks into her studio, takes off his shirt and begs her to help him. Colin Russo needs Demi's healing touch...but having her hands on him is sweet torture!

#715 LIVING THE FANTASY
Kathy Lyons
Ali Flores has never believed in luck, until she accidentally lands a part on a video game tour. Now she's learning all about gaming. But what she *really* likes is playing with hunky company CEO Ken Johnson....

#716 FOLLOW MY LEAD
Stepping Up
Lisa Renee Jones
The host and one of the judges of TV's hottest reality dance show put the past behind them and embark on a sensually wild, emotionally charged fling!

You can find more information on upcoming Harlequin® titles, free excerpts and more at www.Harlequin.com.

HBCNM0912

REQUEST YOUR FREE BOOKS!
2 FREE NOVELS PLUS 2 FREE GIFTS!

✦ Harlequin® *Blaze*™

red-hot reads!

YES! Please send me 2 FREE Harlequin® Blaze™ novels and my 2 FREE gifts (gifts are worth about $10). After receiving them, if I don't wish to receive any more books, I can return the shipping statement marked "cancel." If I don't cancel, I will receive 6 brand-new novels every month and be billed just $4.49 per book in the U.S. or $4.96 per book in Canada. That's a saving of at least 14% off the cover price. It's quite a bargain. Shipping and handling is just 50¢ per book in the U.S. and 75¢ per book in Canada.* I understand that accepting the 2 free books and gifts places me under no obligation to buy anything. I can always return a shipment and cancel at any time. Even if I never buy another book, the two free books and gifts are mine to keep forever.

151/351 HDN FEQE

Name _____ (PLEASE PRINT) _____

Address _____ Apt. # _____

City _____ State/Prov. _____ Zip/Postal Code _____

Signature (if under 18, a parent or guardian must sign)

Mail to the **Reader Service:**
IN U.S.A.: P.O. Box 1867, Buffalo, NY 14240-1867
IN CANADA: P.O. Box 609, Fort Erie, Ontario L2A 5X3

Not valid for current subscribers to Harlequin Blaze books.

Want to try two free books from another line?
Call 1-800-873-8635 or visit www.ReaderService.com.

* Terms and prices subject to change without notice. Prices do not include applicable taxes. Sales tax applicable in N.Y. Canadian residents will be charged applicable taxes. Offer not valid in Quebec. This offer is limited to one order per household. All orders subject to credit approval. Credit or debit balances in a customer's account(s) may be offset by any other outstanding balance owed by or to the customer. Please allow 4 to 6 weeks for delivery. Offer available while quantities last.

Your Privacy—The Reader Service is committed to protecting your privacy. Our Privacy Policy is available online at www.ReaderService.com or upon request from the Reader Service.

We make a portion of our mailing list available to reputable third parties that offer products we believe may interest you. If you prefer that we not exchange your name with third parties, or if you wish to clarify or modify your communication preferences, please visit us at www.ReaderService.com/consumerschoice or write to us at Reader Service Preference Service, P.O. Box 9062, Buffalo, NY 14269. Include your complete name and address.

HARLEQUIN® *Blaze*™

red-hot reads

Two sizzling fairy tales with men straight from your wildest dreams...

Fan-favorite authors

Rhonda Nelson & Karen Foley

bring readers another installment of

Blazing Bedtime Stories, Volume IX

THE EQUALIZER

Modern-day righter of wrongs, Robin Sherwood is a man on a mission and will do everything necessary to see that through, especially when that means catching the eye of a fair maiden.

GOD'S GIFT TO WOMEN

Sculptor Lexi Adams decides there is no such thing as the perfect man, until she catches sight of Nikos Christakos, the sexy builder next door. She convinces herself that she only wants to sculpt him, but soon finds a cold stone statue is a poor substitute for the real deal.

Available October 2012 wherever books are sold.

www.Harlequin.com

HB79715

New York Times *bestselling author Brenda Jackson presents TEXAS WILD, a brand-new Westmoreland novel.*

Available October 2012 from Harlequin Desire®!

Rico figured there were a lot of things in life he didn't know. But the one thing he did know was that there was no way Megan Westmoreland was going to Texas with him. He was attracted to her, big-time, and had been from the moment he'd seen her at Micah's wedding four months ago. Being alone with her in her office was bad enough. But the idea of them sitting together on a plane or in a car was arousing him just thinking about it.

He could tell by the mutinous expression on her face that he was in for a fight. That didn't bother him. Growing up, he'd had two younger sisters to deal with, so he knew well how to handle a stubborn female.

She crossed her arms over her chest. "Other than the fact that you prefer working alone, give me another reason I can't go with you."

He crossed his arms over his own chest. "I don't need another reason. You and I talked before I took this case, and I told you I would get you the information you wanted... doing things my way."

He watched as she nibbled on her bottom lip. So now she was remembering. Good. Even so, he couldn't stop looking into her beautiful dark eyes, meeting her fiery gaze head-on.

"As the client, I demand that you take me," she said.

He narrowed his gaze. "You can demand all you want, but you're not going to Texas with me."

Megan's jaw dropped. "I *will* be going with you since there's no good reason that I shouldn't."

He didn't say anything for a moment. "Okay, there is another reason I won't take you with me. One that you'd do well to consider," he said in a barely controlled tone. She had pushed him, and he didn't like being pushed.

"Fine, let's hear it," she snapped furiously.

He placed his hands in the pockets of his jeans, stood with his legs braced apart and leveled his gaze on her. "I want you, Megan. Bad. And if you go anywhere with me, I'm going to have you."

He then turned and walked out of her office.

Will Megan go to Texas with Rico?

*Find out in Brenda Jackson's brand-new
Westmoreland novel, TEXAS WILD.*

Available October 2012 from Harlequin Desire®.

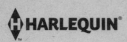

HARLEQUIN®

n○cturne™

Satisfy your paranormal cravings with two dark
and sensual new werewolf tales from
Harlequin® Nocturne™!

FOREVER WEREWOLF
by Michele Hauf

Can sexy, charismatic werewolf Trystan Hawkes win the
heart of Alpine pack princess Lexi Connors—or will dark
family secrets cost him the pack's trust…and her love?

THE WOLF PRINCESS
by Karen Whiddon

Will Dr. Braden Streib risk his life to save royal wolf shifter
Princess Alisa—even if it binds them inescapably together
in a battle against a deadly faction?

> **Plus look for a reader-favorite story
> included in each book!**

2 GREAT NOVELS SAME GREAT PRICE

Available September 18, 2012

www.Harlequin.com

HN88555